The Ship from Simnel Street

THE SHIP FROM SIMNEL STREET

Jenny Overton

GREENWILLOW BOOKS
NEW YORK

Library of Congress Cataloging-in-Publication Data
Overton, Jenny.
The ship from Simnel Street.
Summary: A London baker's daughter runs off to Lisbon to search
for her sweetheart who is fighting in the Peninsular
War, leaving behind a distraught family that concocts a
colossal scheme to demonstrate their support of her action.
[1. Bakers and bakeries—Fiction.   2. London (England)—Social
life and customs—19th century—Fiction]   I. Title.
PZ7.0964Sh   1986   [Fic]   85-21965
ISBN 0-688-06182-6

Contents

1   The Bakery in Simnel Street   9

2   Hark Now the Drum   12

3   In Season to Shear   16

4   The Young and Single Sailor   22

5   Farewell My Joy   30

6   Play the Dead March   38

7   Gone to Serve the King   42

8   Over the Hills and O'er the Main   49

9   Frost on the Down   62

10   It Was on Easter Day   73

11   The King's Birthday   80

12   Making Ready   87

13   The First Baking   94

14   Sugar Under Sail   97

15   The Harbour Side Is Crowded   108

16   From the Far Far Coast of Portugal   113

17   A Lesson Learned   118

18   The Dole Door   122

19   Cradle Cake   127

20   Sung in the Streets   133

Acknowledgements   143

1

The Bakery in Simnel Street

The Oliver family had owned the bakery for over a hundred
years. The shop was in Simnel Street, which ran down to the
Market Place at the heart of the town, and the bakehouse
was built at right angles to it. In earlier years, when
Susannah's grandfather was Master Baker, the family lived
over the shop, but when her father Jonathan took over the
bakery he built a new house to welcome his bride. It was a
neat brick house, three floors high; its back windows
overlooked the yard behind the shop, but it had its own
front door, with a brass knocker and a fanlight and a flight of
half-moon steps, and its own strip of pavement (cobble-
stoned at Jonathan's expense), with a row of trim white
posts to divide it from the street.

The Olivers' daughters, Polly and Susannah, were both
born in the new house, and their mother was determined
that they should have every advantage Jonathan could
afford to give them. Instead of sending them to the Dame
School at a penny a week, he paid a guinea a term for them
to attend a small private school kept by Miss Honeywood, a
clergyman's daughter. He paid for music lessons too, and
bought a piano on which Polly could practise her scales. He
drank coffee for breakfast instead of ale, and gave up eating
his dinner in the kitchen. And on his fifteenth wedding
anniversary he bought his wife a present from Joseph
Gooding, the town's leading tea-dealer: a rosewood caddy
with a pound of green tea in one compartment and a pound

of black tea in the other, and a fitted bowl in which to blend them to her taste. Tea was very fashionable and very expensive, and he could not have chosen anything which would have pleased her more. She at once planned some evening card parties when her daughters could blend and brew and pour out the elegant drink. Polly teased her about it: watching her sip the smoky tea and arrange her face into an approving look, she said, 'Wouldn't you sooner have a mug of ale, Mam love? Something with a bit of strength and comfort to it?'

The first card party was not a success. The kettle sulked, the brew was too strong, the cream was on the turn: even Jonathan's best meringues could not save the occasion. The story soon got out, and up and down the streets the children sang a new song:

> *Polly put the kettle on*
> *Polly put the kettle on*
> *Polly put the kettle on*
> *We'll all have tea.*
>
> *Sukey take it off again*
> *Sukey take it off again*
> *Sukey take it off again*
> *They've all gone away.*

This annoyed Mrs Oliver very much, but she had enough good sense not to bang her parlour window shut, or send out one of the maids to bribe the children into leaving, as other people sometimes did. By the time of her third party, which passed off very well, the town was talking of other things. 'That's right, my love,' said Jonathan, 'pay no attention. You enjoy your tea parties, and that's all that matters.'

'I'd sooner Polly put herself out to enjoy them too,' Mrs Oliver said tartly. 'She's a pretty girl, our Polly, and could do well for herself – why, Mrs Pratt said as much to me, though the words were vinegar in her mouth. But Polly would sooner scorch her face at the bakehouse fire than sit in the parlour and be polite to the callers.'

'Now, Dorothy my dear, I can't bar my own daughters from the bakery.'

'No, but with the business doing well, we could move out of town,' Mrs Oliver said. 'One of those smart new villas on the Eastcliff. You could afford it, my love. Put Abram in charge of the bakery. He and his Pru could live snug and warm in this house, and you could come into town every day, twice or thrice a day if need be, and see all was running smoothly.'

But Jonathan was a townsman born and bred, and he would not move away from Oliver's. He mixed the starter dough every afternoon ready for the next day's baking, and was up before dawn to join Abram Trower, his foreman, and the apprentices at work in the bakehouse. Had he had a son, he would have brought him up to the trade. But he gave way to his wife over Polly and Susannah. Pru Trower, Abram's middle-aged daughter, ran the shop, and the girls were only allowed to help behind the counter on festival days. When they were small, Mrs Oliver would not let them play in the streets ('No daughter of mine is going to be sung through the town as a hoyden'); nor, as they grew older, would she hear of their being apprenticed to one of the milliners or dressmakers in Bugle Street.

She had great plans for her daughters, and the worst day of her life was the one when Polly told her that she wanted to marry a soldier.

2

Hark Now the Drum

The soldier's name was Dick Fletching. He was a rifleman whose company had been sent to garrison the Fort which guarded the Harbour. The Army baked its own bread, but its officers came into town to visit the coffee-houses, order wine and snuff from the local shops, and read the London newspapers. They sometimes dined at Myngs, the best hotel in town, and there the colonel enjoyed Jonathan's fresh-baked macaroons and sent an order to the bakery for a dozen twice weekly. Polly took the first batch to the Fort, and Dick was on duty at the gate. After that they usually contrived to meet once a week, sometimes twice, and Dick got himself assigned to the recruiting party which marched into town on Sunday mornings and paraded in the Market Place before and after church. The sergeant was very ready to allow his men to talk with the local girls, and in spite of Mrs Oliver's disapproval, Polly and Dick managed to get a few minutes to themselves most Sundays.

When the *Courant*, the town's local newspaper, announced that the Regiment had been given its marching orders and that the soldiers at the garrison were to return to their barracks in Kent and there embark for the war in Spain, Mrs Oliver was relieved. 'I daresay they're looking forward to it,' she said firmly. 'Why the French should *want* Spain is more than I can fathom, but the Army will pack them off home again – and good riddance.'

There was no question of Dick's marrying Polly before he

sailed. He had no money and no home. By trade a shepherd, he had lost his place when his master died and the farm was sold up. He had tramped the countryside in search of work, but there were too many other men after every opening. Dreading the risk of being pressganged by the Navy, whose men were trapped aboard ship for years on end, never allowed ashore for fear they would desert, Dick chose instead to join the Army. He was long-sighted, with a shepherd's ability to judge distances well and to take good aim, and this recommended him to the Rifle Brigade.

Polly knew that the chances of his coming home again were small. He might be killed in battle; he might die of wounds, or fever, or exhaustion on the long marches.

'Why did you tell Mam at all, Polly?' Susannah asked one evening. Their parents were playing cards in the Verneys' parlour; the two maids, Harriet and Martha, were putting each other's hair in curl-papers in their bedroom over the bakeshop; and Susannah and Polly were eating a comfortable supper of toasted cheese and preserved plums in the kitchen. 'Why stir up a deal of trouble when it may come to nothing?'

'To stop Mam making plans, of course,' Polly said. 'She's full of hope that I'll marry Kit Tree, or Ben Chartman, or Jack Vere. Or Banker Pratt's nephew. Or that young tailor who's set up shop in Bugle Street. Or, of course, Cousin Henniker. After all,' she said, quoting their mother, 'he has his own grocery and is as respectable a shopman as you'd meet from here to Chichester.' She lined up her plum stones and counted them out:

> Marry a grocer, eat well all your life,
> Marry a cobbler, tread dry as his wife,
> Marry a baker, never lack bread,
> Marry a draper, quilts for your bed.

13

Marry a ploughboy, knee-deep in mire,
Marry a tinker, blackened by fire,
Marry a sailor, salt in your eye,
Marry a soldier, widow you'll die.

'Will you see Dick before he goes?' Susannah asked her.

'Da says I can take a batch of macaroons to the Fort tomorrow, with his compliments to the colonel, so that we can say farewell.'

She went down to the Fort with the macaroons, a loaf of Jonathan's gingerbread for the sergeant on the gate, and an ounce of tobacco for Dick – 'More use to him than money if he's going overseas.' She came back an hour later looking thin and tired. Yes, she had seen Dick. Yes, he was in good health. Yes, the garrison was marching out tomorrow.

The soldiers left at first light, marching away along the cliff road to the shrill sweet music of the fife and the steady beat of the drum. *The Girl I Left Behind Me, Why Soldiers Why,* and *Hark Now the Drum* rang out as they went:

Over the hills and o'er the main
To Shorncliffe, Portugal and Spain,
King George commands and we obey:
Over the hills and far away.

Though Polly knew how to write, Dick did not. The soldiers' pay was, in any case, often months in arrears, and even had he been able to write her a letter, he could seldom spare a penny for the postage. Polly had at first to rely for news on the reports in the *Courant,* and on gossip picked up from the grooms at the coaching inns and the boatmen in the Harbour. But Myngs Hotel took the London newspapers, and the old waiter in the coffee-room said he would save them for her so that she could see up-to-date reports on the war in Spain.

Mrs Oliver said Polly had too much good sense to eat her

heart out. She would get over Dick Fletching, and settle down again. But Susannah knew that Polly had cut the mother-of-pearl buttons off her Sunday gloves, sold them, and spent the money on a map of the Spanish Peninsula at Chartman's Bookshop. She saw her in the bedroom, poring over the newspapers and pencilling the names of the regiments on her map. She did not think Polly would soon forget.

3

In Season to Shear

On the first Saturday in June, Jonathan baked flockbread for the shearing feasts. Susannah woke early and crept downstairs past her mother's door, through the hall and into the silent kitchen. She stepped into the yard. The shop and the store-room and pantry flanking it were in darkness, but the bakehouse glowed with warmth and light. The yard cats crowded its doorstep and fringed the sills of the unshuttered windows. Both Mrs Oliver's brothers were farmers, and despite the bad harvests and the wartime price rises, they kept Jonathan supplied with wheat. The cats had the free run of the grain-store above the pantry, where the sacks of corn were kept, and of the bolting-room, where the apprentices sieved the flour brought home from the town mill, but the boys were forever chasing them out of the warm bakehouse.

The air was fragrant with the live prickling smell of yeast and the dry clean smell of flour. Jonathan was working at the keeler – the deep wooden trough in which the starter dough was left to rise overnight. He had mixed in more flour to make up the dough for the day's baking and was teaching Sam Iden, youngest of his three apprentices, to knead. 'Gently, Sam, gently. Easy as a cat settling to sleep on your knee. That's better. Good lad. Now cover the dough – that's right, a clean warm cloth – and leave it to prove, and if you've done it right, up it'll rise again, light as any dandelion clock.'

Susannah looked at the slate on which Jonathan wrote out the day's orders. Flockbread, rolls, cobs, lardy cakes. Josh Herring, at seventeen the senior apprentice, was trusted with the breakfast rolls. Billy Chennell, fifteen and lively, shaped and proved dough into loaves under Jonathan's eye. 'Sukey love,' Jonathan said, glancing up to see her, 'does your Mam know you're here?'

'She wasn't awake, Da.'

'So you left her to have her sleep out? Very thoughtful. Well, have a word with Abram, and then I daresay you can make yourself useful.'

Abram Trower was tending the ovens, helped by Col, the boy who looked after the brushwood. Jonathan's father had enlarged the bakehouse, building a massive new hearth in the long north wall with two brick ovens, one in either side. Nicknamed 'King Harry' and 'Queen Jane', these ovens took the daily bakings of bread, as well as plum cakes, spice cakes and buns. The old hearth in the west wall dated from the time of Jonathan's grandfather and still had its old-fashioned bakestone. Its bread oven, nicknamed 'Daniel', was kept for the breakfast rolls and, later in the day, for sponge fingers and madeleines and small sweet cakes. Every evening, with the apprentice on duty to help him, Col eased six brushwood bundles through each low arched oven door. At the start of the day's work he set them alight, and by the time the tinder-dry wood had burned away to light hot ash, the oven was at baking heat.

When Susannah came across the bakehouse to greet Abram, he and Col were inspecting 'King Harry'. The fierce heat stopped her in her tracks. Glimpsed through the doorway the bricks were glowing red, and when Abram threw a handful of flour on the oven floor it blazed and blackened in an instant. 'Right, lad,' he said, 'quick now.' Col raked out the hot ash, and there was a gush of steam as he swabbed the oven floor with a wet mop. Abram set-in the loaves with the long-handled peel, Col latched the iron door, and it was time to turn to 'Queen Jane' and begin again. Not until a full batch of flockbreads was baking did Abram have time to wipe his forehead, take a gulp of fresh air and greet Susannah. 'Tasted the flockbread yet, love? Your Da added a spoonful of blackberry jelly this year, and I'm bound to say I reckon it helps the flavour. Break a bit off the tester loaf.'

Susannah was glad to back away from the ovens. Abram had long since been kippered by the heat and smoke, but she felt for young Col as he raked out the ashes and swung the mop. Being a brushwood boy was hard work, but if Col stuck to it Jonathan would take him as an apprentice when Josh completed his seven years, and instead of paying the usual premium, ten guineas, he need only put down ten shillings. Billy Chennell, too, had started work as a brushwood boy – 'And I've got the grey hairs to prove it,' Abram said wryly; 'still, even if he couldn't tell dry gorse from green broom, he was allus a cheerful lad.' Col, on the other hand, was a furze-cutter's son, and knew more about brushwood than Abram himself, but he wasn't used to living in town, or indeed indoors. 'First time I ever had a boy who had to be taught to trim a lamp,' Abram said. 'Still, he's a good lad – reckon he could kindle a fire in a rainstorm.'

Jonathan called to Susannah across the bakehouse: 'If you mark and glaze that last batch, Sukey love – triple slash cut – Billy can start the lardies.'

Billy gave Susannah the knife and went off, whistling, to the pantry to make the lardy cakes. She began to slash three deep cuts across each loaf. 'Cut bold,' Jonathan had told her when first she was allowed to try. 'Better a wrong cut than a weakling.' The cuts would open as the dough proved, and give the bread a crisper crust.

She stamped each loaf with the beechwood marker which carried the Oliver trademark, a clover flower and leaf. Like the bone-handled knife, like the brush to glaze the loaves, it had belonged to Grandfather Oliver, and Jonathan liked to stamp it on anything and everything made in the bakery, even though the mark blurred in the baking.

By now the round cob loaves were proved and ready – 'Checkerboard cut, Sukey.' The breakfast rolls were set-in to bake in 'Daniel'. 'The lardies can wait a while,' Jonathan said. 'Time for a breather. Fetch up the ale, Sam, and see if Miss Pru'd care for a bite.'

They gathered in the bakehouse for fresh hot flockbread, and buttermilk or ale to wash it down: Jonathan himself, Susannah, Abram, Col and the three apprentices; Abram's daughter Pru, who had been setting the shop to rights, ready to take down the shutters as soon as the bread was piped; Polly, coming across the yard to kiss her father's cheek, and the two maids, Harriet and Martha, snatching a few minutes from the kitchen; old Will the yard man, stiff and grizzled as an ageing gundog but with a prizefighter's shoulders; and Josh Herring's young brother Tom, the leader of the delivery boys and always the first to arrive. 'Thirteen of us,' Jonathan said, counting heads. 'Baker's dozen for a baker's table. Set out the flockbread, Sam.'

Made for shepherds and drovers, flockbread was dark and sweet and sustaining, and would stay moist all day long. They cleared half a dozen loaves between them, and Polly said to Susannah, 'If you don't save room for parlour breakfast, Mam will be after you.'

Old Will went away to unbolt the yard gate and let in the rest of the delivery boys. There were twelve in all: two for each of the four town wards, one for St Stephen's, one for the Harbour, and two for the Eastcliff villas. They stowed the rolls and loaves in their baskets, wrapping the bread in clean linen cloths to keep it warm. For each dozen that went into the baskets, one was set aside for the dole which was given away every morning to anyone in need.

'Some people say bakers count thirteen to the dozen for fear of giving short weight and being fined for it,' Jonathan had told his daughters when they were small, 'and others say the thirteenth piece was the boy's wage. But Abram has a different notion.'

'Thirteen at the Last Supper,' Abram said. 'The Saviour and his twelve apostles. Never take money for the thirteenth loaf.'

When she was small, Susannah had enjoyed giving out the dole. Now, though, times were hard, and there was always a line of people waiting in the alley by the dole door: out-of-work labourers, widows with small children, seamen and soldiers wounded in the wars. She and Polly handed out the loaves, saving the rolls for the children. 'Miss Polly,' Martha said, plucking at Polly's sleeve, 'breakfast's laid in't parlour and Missus asking where you be.'

'She knows very well where we are,' Polly said, 'but she doesn't care to admit it. All right, Martha. We're just coming.'

Old Will opened the yard gate and the delivery boys came trooping down the alley, balancing the wide wicker baskets on their heads. Tom Herring was in the lead. As they entered Simnel Street, he began to play the day's tune on his pipe: *Come All My Jolly Boys,* chosen in honour of the shearing feasts. A shutter banged and a woman's voice called, 'There now! Baker's piping his bread, you'll be late to your lessons again.'

The carters and labourers waiting outside the bakeshop to buy flockbread and lardies for the shearing feasts took up the tune, whistling and singing as the boys headed down Simnel Street towards the Market Place:

Come all my jolly boys and we'll together go,
Together with our masters to shear the lambs and yowes.
All in the month of June of all times in the year
It always comes in season the lambs and yowes to shear,
And then we will work hard, my boys, until our backs do break,
Our Master he will bring us beer whenever we do lack.

4

The Young and Single Sailor

Because of the shearing feasts trade was brisk all day, and
Mrs Oliver allowed Polly and Susannah to help in the shop.
That evening they were sitting on the kitchen doorstep,
soaking their tired feet in the washtub, when Cassy
Woodling tapped at the front door. She was Polly's closest
friend, a gentle girl of whom Mrs Oliver thoroughly
approved. Her parents were dead, and she had been
brought up by her grandfather, an apothecary in Green
Street. For nearly two years she had been betrothed to a
young seaman, Will Downer, who was surgeon's mate
aboard the sloop *Benwick*. His ship had made harbour two
weeks earlier, and now, at last, Cassy had had a message
from him.

'I can hardly believe it, but Will promises it's true,' she
told Polly. 'It's come through at last, the prize money for the
French frigate they captured two years since, and Will's
been paid his share, so he spoke to the surgeon, and the
surgeon spoke to the captain, and he's been given leave to
come ashore on Thursday, two days' leave, so that we can
marry. You'll be my bridesmaid, won't you, Polly? And I
have to find the groomsmen too, as Will's shipmates won't
be allowed ashore. I thought of asking Kit Tree – And could I
buy one of your keeper cakes, Mr Oliver? And –'

'No, Cassy,' Mrs Oliver said firmly, overhearing this. 'If
your poor mother was alive, she'd see to it you had a proper
bride-cake. Almond paste and sugar icing and all the

trimmings. So you'll do us the kindness to let us give you the cake you deserve, my dear.'

'Quite right, quite right,' Jonathan said. 'Thursday, you say? Then we'd best make a start tonight. Sukey love, check the store cupboard and walk round to Cousin Henniker's if we're running short. Martha, tell Sam to set my table for a bride-cake baking, and to send word to the other lads. Now, Cassy, what about the wedding waggon? Your granddad's welcome to a loan of our cart.'

Susannah went to the office to look up the bride-cake recipe which her grandfather had copied into the daybook fifty years before, and unlocked the store-room. Jonathan's keeper cakes had a shelf to themselves – two dozen of them, each in its own small wooden box sealed with blobs of wax bearing the bakery trademark; they sold best at Christmas, but there was a steady demand all year round from wealthy customers buying for sons at boarding-school or naval officers going to sea, and townspeople wanting cradle cake for a christening or something to pluck up the mourners after a burial. Below them were the jars of candied peel (Jonathan made his own each summer, ordering sugar loaves and half a dozen crates of oranges and lemons from Cousin Henniker) and the deep drawers of nuts, rice, raisins and other grocery goods. Susannah checked the spice cupboard as well and found they would need mace and cinnamon bark.

She walked down to Cousin Henniker's grocery in Green Street. It was a trim, well-kept shop and smelled delicious. Mrs Oliver approved of Cousin Henniker – 'He would make Polly an excellent husband, and he'd be a good son-in-law besides'; Jonathan, though, said he aged three years for every one he lived. When she got back to Simnel Street, Sam was in the bakehouse setting out Jonathan's tools: spoons, knives, steel sharpener, pestle and mortar, nutmeg grater, sugar-loaf grippers and cutters, basins, jugs, the dented silver dish and big fork he kept for beating eggs, the sieves ranging in size from five inches to fifty and in mesh from wire to finest silk, the largest baking hoop, the parchment and scissors, the apothecary scales used for measuring powdered spices and the vast Doomsday scales which were large enough to weigh a full peck of flour.

'It's hard luck on you, Sam, having an order tonight,' she said. Saturday was usually the quietest night of the week since Jonathan did not bake on Sundays. The brick ovens took all day and all night to cool, and many families brought Sunday's dinner to the bakehouse on Saturday evening and handed it over to bake slowly in the dying heat. The duty apprentice collected their pennies and kept an eye on who brought what, in case of arguments when the dishes were reclaimed next day, but that apart, he could usually sleep peacefully on the truckle bed until dawn, and beyond.

Sam said, 'Oh well, seems Thursday's short notice for a bride-cake.' He was looking anxiously at the table, wondering if he had remembered everything.

The other boys arrived, and Jonathan came in, rolling up his sleeves. 'Two hours' work and a shilling a-piece,' he said. 'Billy, you and Sam pick over the currants – clean as a whistle, mind – and stone the raisins.'

Billy made a face but said, 'Yes, sir.'

'Josh, you blanch and shred the almonds. Now, Sukey my dear, does your Mam know you're here? Step over to the house and be sure she approves, and on your way send Martha, if Harriet can spare her.' As he spoke, he was cracking eggs, deftly dropping the yolks in one bowl, the whites in another. He sat down with the old silver dish on his lap and began beating the whites with his fork.

Two hours later, the bowls ranged along the worktable were piled high: clean black currants, damp raisins tossed in flour, sticky peel chopped into fragments, almonds like slips of ivory, glossy candied cherries. The flour had been

24

sifted to extract the bran, and sifted a second time through silk; the sugar chopped up, crushed, sifted twice; the butter beaten soft with a wooden spoon; the spices freshly ground; the egg whites beaten to foam. Col had fired 'King Harry' and reported it ready; Sam had buttered and lined the baking hoop. Josh and Billy went off home, jingling their extra shillings; Jonathan and Sam stayed hard at work.

At dawn on Sunday morning Jonathan took the cake out of the oven, rich and dark and spicy. Susannah looked into the pantry to admire it. She found Sam fast asleep on the truckle bed in the bakehouse. 'Go home, Sam,' she said, shaking him awake. 'Your Mam will be fretting. I'll deal with the dinners.'

A stream of women called at the dole door to reclaim their dishes of salt pork and beans, mutton and pearl barley, rabbit and onions. They were full of questions. Was it true Dorcas Woodling was marrying her sailor at last? When was the wedding? Was Baker making the bride-cake?

On Monday Abram made the almond paste and coated the cake, while Jonathan crushed the sugar and Billy whistled at the sieve. On Wednesday they mixed the icing, spread it over the cake, and left it to dry on the bakehouse table, swathed like a beekeeper in protective veils of gauze. Susannah chose three of the gingerbread moulds from the office chest – the true-love knot and the dove, as usual for a wedding and, as a compliment to the bridegroom, the anchor – and Josh made the gingerbread favours which Cassy and Will would give to their well-wishers on their wedding journey round the town.

Polly had planned to wear the cotton gown she kept for church on Sundays, but Mrs Oliver went to Osborne's, the best drapery in town, and spent two guineas on a dress-length of yellow muslin; and with her friends to help her, Polly managed to get it cut out, tacked and stitched in time.

On Thursday morning, Kit Tree, the chief groomsman, arrived in Simnel Street with the wedding ribbons. 'For your apprentices, sir,' he said giving Jonathan a bunch.

'Where's the other groomsmen, Kit?'

'Waiting for the groom at the Sea Gate. They reckon it's too risky to go down to the Harbour.'

Mrs Oliver said, 'They've got their certificates, haven't they, exempting them from sea service?'

'Times the Navy don't stop to ask,' Kit said.

Jonathan nodded. 'War's getting closer,' he said.

Polly came downstairs in the yellow muslin. 'Careful now, don't crease the skirt,' Mrs Oliver said. 'Mind the handrail. If those are your best gloves, what became of the buttons Aunt Soper sent you?'

Kit said, 'You look prime, Polly love.' He gave her a bunch of wedding ribbons and she pinned them to her bodice.

'And you look a proper fashion-plate,' she said, teasing him gently.

'Now, Polly, where's your bonnet?' Mrs Oliver said. 'I thought that girl at the milliner's was fresh-trimming it for you –'

'Barbary Chance, yes. She was, she did, and it's on the parlour table,' Polly said.

She fetched the bonnet and came into the hall swinging it blithely from her hand.

'*Careful*, you'll crush the ribbons. Well, I suppose you'll do. Our love to Cassy, and we'll see her in church. Watch where you tread, now. Take good care of her, Kit – if I see a speck of dirt on that new muslin, I'll box your ears.'

Sam and Col had decorated the cart with branches of broom, and Billy had looped white ribbons exuberantly round it. Josh and Abram carried out the cake, swathed in butter-muslin to protect it from dust, flies and sticky fingers, and wedged it into place with flour sacks. Old Will hitched up the pony and clambered on to the box. Josh

26

handed out the wedding ribbons. 'Tie mine to the whip, lad,' Will said. 'If'n I drive up to Church with my face clean-shaven and wedding ribbons round my sleeve, they'll take me for the groom himself.'

The girls had picked wild flowers for Cassy's wedding garland which was hanging on the church door. It was made of young green ivy, set with knots of the starry white stitchwort which people nicknamed Sailors Buttons.

Cassy's friends and neighbours were waiting at the steps, and there was a little crowd of onlookers in the Market Place, eager to see if the groom would be allowed ashore. They gave him a ragged cheer as he emerged from Fore Street in his blue jacket, wide trousers and straw hat, escorted by Kit Tree and the other groomsmen, all with wedding ribbons fluttering from their sleeves. 'Thanks be,' said Mrs Oliver. 'Time we went in.'

Bridegroom, groomsmen and Parson took their places. There was a stir and bustle at the back of the church as the apprentices led in the bride, on her grandfather's arm. Polly was behind her, in the new yellow muslin. When Parson said, 'Say after me, "I Dorcas take thee William to my wedded husband",' Susannah looked sideways at her mother and saw her thinking, plain as print, of Polly in Cassy's place, saying, 'I Mary take thee –' But whom did she see as the groom? Cousin Henniker? Kit Tree? Young Mr Pratt?

The guests streamed across the Market Place to enjoy the wedding-breakfast at the Agamemnon. The busiest of the town's coaching inns, it had been named for the British flagship, but its sign showed a naval officer brandishing his sword and the townspeople promptly nicknamed it 'Egg the Men On'; from Portsmouth to Deal it was now known simply as The Egg. In The Egg's coffee-room the party drank long life to Will and Cassy, victory to King George and confusion to the French. Then Mrs Oliver picked up the cake knife, and the other women shushed the children and frowned the men into quiet as she put it in Cassy's right hand, and reached for Will's hand and closed it over his bride's. 'There now, my dear,' she said, as Cassy's mother would have done had she been there, 'cut your cake, and may you never go hungry.' There was a scattering of applause as Will and Cassy cut the cake and Polly carried round the slices. Then the fiddler struck up *Brighton Camp*, and while the young men and girls danced in the passage, the older women untied their bonnet strings and eased their feet out of their shoes, and the men settled down to talk of the war, until it was time for Cassy and Will to set out on their journey round the town.

Usually the wedding waggon carried the bride to her new home with a great heap of household goods piled behind her (Mrs Oliver had been laying aside blankets, towels, pots and pans, china and cutlery, since the day Polly was born). But as Cassy was returning to her grandfather's house, she had only to take the baskets of gingerbread favours. Kit Tree swung himself up on the box and flourished the whip. The groomsmen boosted Will over the tailgate and Cassy's grandfather handed her up to sit beside him. Mrs Oliver gave her a great wedge of bride-cake, according to custom – 'For your first meal as man and wife, my dear, and may it bring you blessing.' Then, to a cheer from the potboys and the waiters, the waggon rumbled out of The Egg's yard to circle the Market Place. Led by Polly, the girls linked hands and followed it, singing the song they had chosen as their own farewell to Cassy. It was *The Young and Single Sailor*, and Cassy blushed as the onlookers whistled the tune:

> *A fair maid walked all in her garden,*
> *A brisk young sailor she chanced to spy,*
> *He stepped up to her thinking to view her,*
> *Says he, 'Fair maid could you fancy me?'*

'Oh no, young man, I have a sweetheart,
And seven long years he's away from me,
And seven more I will wait for him,
And if he's alive he will return to me –'

'Oh seven years makes an alteration,
Perhaps he's drowned and is now at rest –'
'Then no other man shall ever join me,
For he's the darling boy that I love best.'

He put his hand all in his pocket,
His fingers being both long and small,
Saying, 'Here's the ring, love, we broke between us –'
Soon as she saw it, then she down did fall.

He took her close all in his arms,
He gave her kisses one two three,
Saying, 'I'm your young and single sailor
That has come home for to marry thee.'

The waggon turned into Fore Street, taking the longest
way home, and Cassy threw her nosegay to Polly who
caught and flourished it, laughing. Children ran alongside
the waggon, singing *Cupid's Garden* for Cassy, and reaching
up for the gingerbread favours. Men and women came to
their doors to wish the bride luck and give the groom free
advice. The wedding guests followed, led by the groomsmen and the girls, but Polly and several of Cassy's close
friends slipped away. While the waggon trundled slowly
round the town, they went to the apothecary's house in
Green Street, to light the kitchen fire, hang the kettle over it,
spread the cloth on the table, put fresh candles in the
candlesticks. Last of all, Polly tied up the door-knocker with
her bunch of wedding ribbons. 'There,' she said, 'and let's
hope the Navy leaves them in peace.'

5

Farewell My Joy

Will went aboard two days later. Cassy had spent ten shillings of her savings on comforts for his bundle (tobacco, warm stockings, Jonathan's lemon-flavoured sugar drops), and her grandfather added a bottle of wine from Bonallack's, the best wine merchant in town, for the surgeon. *Benwick* left harbour on the morning tide.

'Along the Hard they're saying she's carrying dispatches down Channel,' Abram told Polly. '*Old Cumberland's* still in harbour 'n *Royal Sussex* likewise. Reckon she'll be back inside a week.'

'Fingers crossed for Cassy's sake,' Polly said.

Jonathan baked little gooseberry tarts, shaped like miniature turrets, to sell at the Midsummer Fair in St Stephen's Fields. Polly and Susannah wandered among the stalls. When the fiddlers struck up a country dance, Banker Pratt's nephew came over to Polly and asked, a little stiffly, if she would do him the honour; Mrs Oliver nodded and smiled, gratified to see them talking comfortably as they waited in the line of dancers. There was a new recruiting party from the Fort – lieutenant, sergeant, troopers in scarlet coats – but to her relief Polly paid them no attention. Kit Tree came across the grass to greet Susannah and her mother, and to warn them of rumours in his father's yard that the Press Gang would soon be out in force. Shipyard workers were exempt, and had certificates to prove it; apprentices, too, were supposed to be safe, but Mrs Oliver and Susannah vividly recalled the disappearance of Abram's godson three years earlier. Eighteen years old, fresh from completing his apprenticeship at Oliver's, he set out one Sunday to see his girl who lived in one of the villages up-river, and never came back. 'Warn your lads to take care,' Kit said, 'at least until *Cumberland* and *Sussex* clear harbour. Polly looks well. She's giving that yellow dress another airing, I see.'

'Young Mr Pratt talked her into dancing,' Mrs Oliver said.

Kit grinned. 'I daresay she didn't take much persuading – and just as well, seeing all he ever does is repeat his uncle's opinions.'

'They're talking very amiably,' Mrs Oliver said, 'and I'm happy to see it.'

Polly danced with Cousin Henniker, with Kit himself, and again with young Mr Pratt, before rejoining her mother and sister. On the way home they paused to buy a bunch of roses from one of the gardener's barrows and took them to the old graveyard which lay outside the town walls, sheltered by the great West Rampart. There were posies on most of the graves, and a few had 'Midsummer cushions' of green turf stuck with flowers and leaves. They left the roses on the grave of the Oliver grandparents and walked home through the quiet streets to find Jonathan dozing over the *Courant* in the parlour. Harriet and Martha had both been given leave to go to the Fair but arrived home soon after. 'Fair's turning rowdy,' Harriet said. 'Allus does come dusk. The lads started rolling empty casks down the Fields into t'river, and I reckoned they might pop Martha inside one for the fun a' hearing her squeal. If you'll unlock the tea caddy, Missus, us can brew a pot a' parlour tea to go with your supper tray.'

They were sitting over their tea in the parlour when a bunch of children ran down Simnel Street towards the Market Place, singing at the tops of their voices:

All things are quite silent, each mortal at rest,
When me and my love got snug in one nest,
But a bold set a' ruffians they entered our cave
And they forced my dear jewel to plough the salt wave.

Jonathan sat up abruptly. 'Press Gang warning,' he said. 'Sukey, run to the bakehouse. I'll check the shop.'

I begged hard for my sailor as though I begged for my life,
They'd not listen to me although a fond wife,
Saying 'The King he wants sailors, to the sea he must go,'
And they've left me lamenting in sorrow and woe.

Susannah ran across the yard. Josh was duty apprentice. She found him checking the bolts on the yard gate.

'All's safe, I reckon,' he said. 'Col went home a few minutes since, but he's such a shrimp the Press wouldn't take him even if he ran slap into their arms. Best check the dole door, too. Not that I think they'd break in, but better safe than sorry.'

'Does your Tom still mean to volunteer, Josh?'

'Aye, the minute he turns twelve. Our Da won't let him go sooner.'

'You don't hanker after the sea yourself?' Susannah asked him.

'I'm not a baker born,' Josh said, 'not like your Da. But the work's snug come winter, and feeds you well all year round, and I wouldn't want for better. Besides, with Tom mad keen to see the world, and Ned so frail he'll never make old bones, one of us should be in a safe trade. Baking suits me fine and allus has.'

Polly came into the bakehouse. 'Martha's in floods of tears fretting over her brothers,' she said, 'and Harriet's mopping her up. It's a wicked thing, the Press, and no one will make me think different, for all their fine words.'

'Who's been saying what, precisely?' Susannah asked.

'Oh well, it was young Mr Pratt. "My uncle says the

King's ships must needs be manned or what will become of us all",' she quoted, '"and if men won't go willing, what else can the Navy do?" So I said it was neither just nor merciful, and if the Navy would pay its men prompt and fair, and feed and clothe them decent, we'd all get on a deal better. He coloured up, poor lad, and stammered out something about not wishing to offend. He means well – I shouldn't have fired up at him.'

On Sunday morning the town was buzzing with the news that three men were missing from St Andrew's (poorest and most crowded of the town wards), one from St Nicholas, and six from the villages up-river. 'Three labourers lodging in Duck Yard,' old Will told Susannah, 'too fuddled with beer to take to their heels in time. And a young wheelwright from the coach-builder's in Rider Street. Word is they took a shopman too, one of Joseph Gooding's men, but he took so high and mighty a tone, claiming he was first cousin to Mr Mayor himself, that they thought better of it. *Royal Sussex* sailed on the morning tide, and it's a pound to a penny the other lads were aboard her. Danger's not past yet, neither – *Admiral Crawford* made harbour this morning, and has the flagship's berth, and *Lord Protector*'s expected come the morrow.'

On Monday Susannah walked down Fore Street to the Sea Gate and climbed the ramparts on her way to school. The wind tugged at her bonnet as she walked along, looking down on the boats in the Inner Harbour and the King's ships at anchor in the Outer Harbour beyond. She saw *Admiral Crawford* in the flagship's berth but not, as yet, *Lord Protector*. Far out to sea was a transport, wallowing down Channel. As she sat in Miss Honeywood's parlour, working a line of featherstitch on a sampler for her Aunt Soper, she wondered if Dick Fletching was aboard that transport on his way to Spain.

On her way home that afternoon she called at Myngs

33

Hotel, to see if the old waiter had any news for Polly. 'It don't look too good for your sister, Susannah love,' he told her. 'I couldn't take no Bible oath, mind, but I heard 'em talking, the stiff-necked commodore we've got staying at present, and an Admiralty clerk that's bobbing in his wake, and seems the Army's shipping lads to Spain faster'n a cook shells peas.'

Arriving home with this news, Susannah found that Polly had taken advantage of the warm summer wind and washed all the bakehouse linen. The yard was criss-crossed with lines, two hundred cloths and napkins were blowing in the breeze, and old Will's cats, hating the drips and puddles on the cobbles, were sitting along the wall like so many sentries, stiff and staring. Susannah gave her the message, and she bit her lip and said, 'If I only knew –' She refused to say anything more, but after supper she set up a trestle table outside the kitchen door, put the flat-irons to heat, and gathered up the washing, and when Susannah said, 'Don't worry, I can give Harriet a hand – you did all the wash-house work, after all,' she shook her head. 'No, Sukey love, I'm better working.'

Mrs Oliver was marking linen in the parlour while Jonathan sat at the table, writing up the daybook; but the rest of the household was in the yard. Polly and Harriet shared out the ironing; Susannah helped Martha to top and tail a basket of gooseberries; Billy sat on the bakehouse door-step, drawing cartoons on the order slate; Col was polishing his flint elf-bolts on his sleeve – they were his own special luckpieces, gathered on the Downs the day before he set out to take up the job of brushwood boy; old Will pacified his cats with a bucket of fish-heads. The wind had dropped and the light was fading. A young owl swept across the yard, hooting as it went. 'Go home, little cousin,' Polly said, glancing up. 'Go home to your Mammy.'

She saw Martha look puzzled, and said, 'The owl's a

baker's daughter, Martha – didn't you know? Ask Mr Trower to tell you the story some time.'

'Go on now,' Harriet said. 'Tell her yourself.'

'Well then,' Polly said, propping her iron on the door-scraper, 'once there was a baker, and he had a daughter – a pretty girl, but heartless. One winter's night the baker was in the bakehouse shaping the loaves, and our Saviour came to the door and said could he maybe come in and get warm. And the baker said yes, of course, and there'd be a fresh-baked loaf to his supper besides. And he took a double handful of dough and told his daughter to bake a loaf for the stranger while he went to fetch more wood. Well, no sooner was he through the door than his daughter pulled the lump of dough in half, and pulled one of the halves in half again, and so on until she had a bit of dough no bigger than a plum. She tossed that scrap of dough in the oven and she turned our Saviour out of the bakehouse, to wait outside in the cold. But when she opened the oven door ten minutes later, that bit of dough had swelled into a great quartern loaf, four pounds weight and more. Her eyes went round with amazement and set fast in her face, her mouth fell open and she hooted in wonder, her hair turned to feathers and her fingers to claws, and out she flew into the night, calling as she went. And that's what she's been doing ever since.' And she picked up the iron and touched it with one fingertip. 'I'd best put this to heat again. Give me yours too, Harriet.' She went into the house.

Someone came up Simnel Street, singing – a man's voice, not a gang of children, but none the less they listened anxiously for a moment. Then Harriet let go her pent-up breath. 'No need to fret,' she said, 'that's nobbut a pedlar or a ballad-singer.'

Polly brought out a freshly heated iron for Harriet. 'Mam wants me to sit in the parlour,' she said. 'Can you manage without me?'

A few minutes later there was a rap at the yard gate. Will went to answer it, and came stumping across the yard to say it was a pedlar, asking to speak to Baker's daughter. 'Treat him civil, Susannah,' Harriet said, 'I don't fancy telling your Mam there's another owl gone flitting over the rooftops.'

The pedlar was a spry, weatherbeaten man with a bundle of song-sheets under his arm. 'Tuppence a-piece, new as hot cakes,' he said.

'I daresay,' Susannah said, 'but I don't have twopence to spare.'

The pedlar grinned. 'I was a-comin' through Kent a week since,' he said, 'met a rifleman Sandgate way and he said if I called here with a bit of a message for Baker's daughter, there'd be sixpence in it for me.'

Susannah said quickly, 'I'll call my sister.'

But it wasn't easy to winkle Polly out of the parlour. 'A pedlar?' Mrs Oliver said. 'No need to encourage *them* to come calling. He'll be hopping with fleas, and light-fingered into the bargain. Will didn't let him in?'

'No, no, he's out in the alley. Polly was saying she needs pins.'

'Oh, very well. But *don't* let him sweet-talk Martha.'

Polly put down the bread-bag on which she was working the bakery trademark in red cotton thread, and followed Susannah into the kitchen. She said mildly, 'My workbox is fair bristling with pins.'

'He's brought a message from Dick.'

Polly ran across the yard. The others stayed back (Martha sighing in sympathy) so that she could get her message in privacy, but they need not have troubled. It wasn't written, of course, but nor was it spoken, as they had expected. The pedlar simply leant against the gatepost and began to sing a favourite street-corner song, *The Cuckoo*:

I do wish I was a scholar
And could handle of my pen,
There is one private letter
To my true love I would send:
I would send and let you know, my love,
My sorrow, grief and woe,
And may blessings attend you
Wherever you may go.

He followed this with *The Turtle Dove,* a song men sang at work in the fields and the yards, and in the alehouses at night:

Farewell my joy and heart's delight
I must leave you for a while,
Though I go away I will come again
If it be ten thousand mile, my dear,
If it be ten thousand mile.

6

Play the Dead March

A week later *Benwick* limped into harbour with shot-holes in her planking and her foremast cut away. Cassy packed a parcel of ointments and bandages for the surgeon and paid a boatman double fee to row her out to the ship. She was not, of course, allowed on board, but a sailor lowered a bucket for the parcel. She tucked a twist of tobacco under the string and called Will's name up to him, but he made no sign.

Abram Trower had friends among the boatmen and on the following day he brought the latest news to the bakery. *Benwick* had been attacked by a French man-of-war. She had got clear, but being badly damaged had turned for home. Four men had been killed in the attack and a dozen wounded, five of whom had since died.

Cassy bore up well under the news, sure that one of Will's shipmates would have passed her word, had he been among the dead. 'Cousin Henniker told your sister she's sitting quiet and saying not a word,' Jonathan said to Susannah.

'She shows good sense,' Mrs Oliver said approvingly.

Susannah found Polly in the wash-house, rubbing shirts hard on the washboard as if to relieve her feelings. 'If I were Cassy,' she said, banging the wet linen up and down in the suds, 'I wouldn't play mouse in Green Street.'

'What else could she do?'

'Go down to the harbour again. Row out to *Benwick*.'

'They'd never let her on board.'

'I daresay. I'd row round the ship,' Polly said, 'and I'd sing as loud and as long as I could, and pray he'd whistle in answer.'

That evening old Mr Woodling called at the bakery. *Benwick*'s surgeon had sent him word that Will had been badly wounded in the attack, and fever had set in. Next morning, early, came news that Will had died in the night. *Benwick*'s captain had agreed to send his body ashore for burial.

'Ten o'clock at the Sea Gate,' Polly told Jonathan. 'Can you be there, Da? I ought to stay with Cassy.'

'Of course, of course,' Jonathan said. 'And the apprentices, too. We'll make a bit of a show for the poor lad – pipe, drum 'n all.'

Susannah said, 'Can't I go too, Mam?'

Mrs Oliver hesitated. 'Well, there won't be many to follow him. Take a handful of lavender from the garden. If you fetch your bonnet, I'll change the ribbons for you.'

Shortly before ten o'clock they went down Fore Street to the Sea Gate: Susannah in her black-ribboned bonnet, Jonathan and Abram in black hatbands, the apprentices with black ribbons tied round their sleeves. Several young men came down the street to join them – Ben Chartman from the bookshop, Jack Vere from Pratt's Bank in Trumper Street, Kit Tree; all of them had been among Will's groomsmen.

They looked down the Sea Steps to where old Mr Woodling waited, far below. A boat crept across the Harbour. The boatmen lifted Will's body ashore, wrapped in sailcloth, and carried it slowly up the long flights of steps. Mr Woodling followed after. Josh and Billy dragged the burial cart out of the gatehouse, Col tucked the tabor drum under his arm, Sam took the bakehouse pipe out of his pocket.

The Sea Gate was always busy, but it fell quiet for a moment as the boatmen tramped through the gateway. They laid Will's body on the cart. The sailcloth creaked as it settled round him. Susannah scattered the stalks of sweet lavender over the weatherstained shroud, and old Mr Woodling spread Cassy's wedding handkerchief over Will's unseen face.

Jonathan nodded to Col, and the boy set off down Fore Street, tapping the drum. The boatmen hauled the cart after him, and the little group of mourners followed. Carters reined-in to let them pass, touching their hats to the dead man. Sam began to play *The Young Seaman*:

As I was a-walking one midsummer morning,
As I was a-walking along the highway,
Who should I see but my own sailor comrade
With his head wrapped in linen on a bright summer's day.

Come six of his comrades to carry his coffin,
Come girls of the city to follow him on,
And each of you bring a bunch of red roses
To smell all so sweet as we bear him along.

And muffle the drum and play the fife lowly,
Play the dead march in the funeral time,
Then go to your homes and think on that sailor,
Here goes a young seaman cut down in his prime.

Cassy's wedding handkerchief lifted in the light airs as if Will had spread it over his face and fallen asleep on a summer afternoon. Susannah looked away.

They crossed the Market Place, where Parson came to join them, and turned the corner into Green Street. The apothecary's shop was closed and shuttered, the knocker tied up with black ribbon. Cassy and Polly were waiting on the doorstep to join the last stage of the journey. As the little procession passed the grocery, Cousin Henniker came out, tying a bit of black ribbon to the latch as a sign to any customers, and fell into step beside Jonathan. Other neighbours were doing the same.

They went through the little Laystow Gate into the hummocky graveyard. Sexton had dug a grave in the Woodlings' family plot. The men lowered Will's body into it. Parson said the last prayers.

7

Gone to Serve the King

On St Swithin's Day, the fifteenth of July, the Mayor gave a supper for the town's principal tradesmen and the parish officials. It was a grey rainy day, and Jonathan fretted over his chocolate pies and his spun-sugar baskets full of cherries; getting them to the Town Hall intact, and unmarked by the spatters of rain, was not easy. Mrs Oliver, though, approved of the weather, for Banker Pratt's nephew had met Polly in the Market Place and offered her the shelter of his umbrella up Simnel Street, and on the following Sunday he asked her if she would care to stroll on the ramparts after Morning Service.

August came, bringing Lammas, the festival of the 'first loaf'. The Mayor, the Town Clerk, Parson, Farmer Standing who rented the glebe fields, Miller Challen from the town mill, and Jonathan himself, all went off together to cut and grind the corn growing on the Lammas land. They arrived at the bakehouse late that afternoon, sleepy and cheerful from the cider they'd been swigging to help the work along, to watch Jonathan mix the dough for the Lammas loaves. Afterwards they sat on for a couple of hours, mopping up the cider with bread and cheese. Polly and Susannah could hear them singing.

'They sound happy,' Polly said.

'They could have had a nice cold supper in the parlour,' Mrs Oliver said disapprovingly. 'Patties. Syllabubs. Buttered oranges. Raisin wine and the best tea. But no, there they sit in the bakehouse, eating like ploughboys – yes, and drinking like waggoners. Parson, too! He should know better.'

The Lammas loaves came out of the oven, golden brown and smelling delicious. Jonathan packed them into two big baskets which Parson and Mayor carried away to the almshouses. He came back to the house yawning hugely, and fell asleep in the parlour. 'He'll be stiff as a board come morning,' Mrs Oliver said, 'but there's no getting him upstairs in this condition, so he must needs suffer. Fetch a quilt, Polly, and then leave him be.'

By Sunday evening Jonathan was himself again. 'And just as well,' Mrs Oliver said. 'We're starting the jam-making tomorrow, and I can't spare Martha to run up and downstairs tending a man who brought his troubles on himself.'

When Susannah came home from school on Monday, the kitchen windows were wide open, with screens of butter-muslin tacked to the frames, and pots of mignonette ranged along the sills to keep away the flies.

Mrs Oliver was stirring the jam pan over the fire, Harriet washing jars and Martha cleaning a mound of currants. All three were hot, tired and sticky. 'Have you seen your sister, Susan?' Mrs Oliver asked as soon as Susannah came in.

'Not since breakfast, Mam.'

'She's walked round to see Cassy, I suppose, and never a word to me first. Six bushels of fruit to cope with, and like to spoil if it isn't turned into jam today – and that I won't have. See if you can find her.'

Susannah went to Green Street, and Cassy came to the door looking thin and ill. No, she said, she hadn't seen Polly all day. Susannah went across the street to the grocery, to ask Cousin Henniker. 'Perhaps she's gone calling in Trumper Street,' he said, as if the words tasted sour in his mouth.

43

'But why? None of her friends –' Susannah broke off. 'No,' she said, 'I don't think so. There's Peggy Verney, though, or Kitty Osborne, or Fanny Challen.'

'You could try the milliner's,' Cousin Henniker said. 'Madam Henriette's. Polly might have called in for a word with the Chance girl – she likes her, for all her bold ways.'

Susannah thought this was worth trying. She cut through the alley to Bugle Street, slipped into the milliner's where Madam herself and both her girls were waiting on a demanding client, and tapped at the workroom door, to find Barbary in a trying mood. '*I* have to earn my bread,' she said, snapping her scissors under Susannah's nose, 'and I'm behind-hand with this bonnet, thanks to being laid up with a headache half the morning, and Madam like to dock my pay if these ribbon roses aren't done on time – *there* now, that was all it needed!' She had run the needle into her finger. 'If I get blood on this ribbon, there'll be the Devil to pay. I've no notion where your Polly may be, but you could try Trumper Street by all I've heard of her doings lately.' She sucked the blood from her finger and twisted a bit of rag round it. 'Shut the door behind you.'

Susannah came home empty-handed, to find her mother stirring the jam with one hand and reaching for the skimmer with the other. Mrs Oliver clicked her tongue at the news and said, 'Well, you must help in her stead. Find a pinafore, put your hair up, and for goodness' sake make haste.'

Susannah went into Polly's room searching for hairpins, but the chest of drawers and the wash-stand were bare. She looked around in surprise. Where was Polly's hairbrush? Her comb? Her cake of soap? The candlestick was on the stool by her bed, but her tinderbox had gone. So had her needlecase, her penknife, her Bible, the cluster of shell flowers Dick had bought her at the Mayday Fair –

Susannah stood still for a moment. Then, slowly, she began to search for a note. There was nothing in Polly's

44

room, nothing in her own, nothing in their parents'. Downstairs, then. And there, indeed, she found it. On the parlour table, propped against the tea caddy, was a folded note. Susannah put it in her pocket and went into the kitchen.

Mrs Oliver said, 'Did you fall asleep up there? Quick now, before the jam catches –' She looked more closely at her daughter. 'Are you feeling poorly, child? Yes, I can see you are. Sit down, do. Martha, fetch me a cup of water, and make haste.'

'Not me, Mam – it's Polly.'

'Polly's ill? You should have called me. Harriet, stir the pan for me – never mind those dratted jars.'

Susannah followed her mother into the hall. 'Wait, Mam,' she said, 'please wait. I found this.'

As Mrs Oliver read the note, all the colour faded from her face, leaving it whitish brown and lifeless. She sat down on the stairs. 'Your father,' she said. 'Where is he?'

Susannah ran to the bakehouse. Jonathan wasn't there. He wasn't in the pantry, the office, the store-room or the shop. She found him at last upstairs in the whitewashed bolting-room, whistling as he sieved bran out of the new-milled flour.

'Can you come, Da? It's Mam. She's desperate upset.'

'Upset?' Jonathan said. 'Over what? Where is she?'

Mrs Oliver was still sitting on the stairs. Jonathan helped her to her feet and took her into the parlour. Susannah sat down to wait. Presently her father came out and gave her Polly's note.

> I am going to try to find Dick. I can't bear to sit at home and not know what is happening to him. Don't let Cassy think this is due to her and Will, I made up my mind weeks since. Believe me none the less your loving Polly.

Where had she gone, and how? 'She must have taken the

45

Stage to Chichester,' Jonathan said. 'Then either up to London, or cross country to the West. I'll take tomorrow's Stage. Sukey, send the boy for Abram. Make some excuse – an urgent order for tomorrow –'

Mrs Oliver said, 'No. Word will get out fast enough.'

'Dorothy my dear, I'll have her home in no time. We can say she's gone to visit Sister Soper in London –'

'No. You'll need to ask questions. Better to be open.'

Susannah sent Col to fetch Abram and came back to the house to find her father questioning Harriet and Martha.

'She helped Miss Pru in the shop for an hour or so, sir,' Harriet said, 'but I don't know where she went after that.'

Mrs Oliver said, 'She was at breakfast. I saw her at breakfast.'

'Yes, my dear, yes, but after that –'

Martha said, 'I saw her, sir, with my own eyes, mid morning, going over the yard in her cloak, her grey cloak, and I wondered a bit, with sun shining fit to burst, but then I reckoned she was going to see Mrs Cassy and wanted to look sad-like –'

'Yes, Martha, yes. Was she carrying a cloakbag?'

'Didn't see none, sir.'

'Well, I'll try the coach office first – Is that Abram's voice? We're in a deal of trouble, Abram, and the Lord alone knows how it's to be put to rights.'

Abram looked as if he had aged ten years.

'Sit down, old friend,' Jonathan said. 'Where's that boy? Col, fetch a glass of brandy wine for Mr Trower, and quick about it – no, Abram, no arguing – and after that, Col lad, ask Mr Henniker to step round, we owe it to him to tell him ourselves. Now, Martha, run to Pratt's Bank, and ask Mr Pratt if I could call to see him this evening – I have to go away on urgent family business, and would be much obliged for a word. Harriet, pack a bag for me, there's a good girl. And

Sukey, take care of your Mam. I'll be back as soon as ever I can.'

Abram drank his brandy and looked the better for it. He took himself off to the bakehouse to mix the starter dough for the following day. Susannah was left in the parlour with her mother. They sat in silence, not a word between them as they waited.

Polly had booked a seat on the Chichester Stage two days earlier, at The Egg's coach-office.

'North to London,' Jonathan said, 'or west to Bath. The Lisbon packet sails from Falmouth – Well, I'm certain to pick up the trail in Chichester. Don't fret yourself, Dorothy my dear. I'll have her home in no time.'

Abram would neither accept a bed in the house nor go home to sleep: he dozed in the bakehouse through the night hours, and was at work well before dawn. Jonathan came across the yard, too tired and anxious to sleep, and joined Billy at the keeler. They baked, as usual, bread and rolls and buns, working without a word. The other boys arrived soon after, very subdued.

When the delivery boys arrived, Tom Herring whispered to Josh, 'Ought us to pipe today?'

Josh hesitated, but Jonathan had overheard.

'Pipe as usual, Tom.'

'Yes, sir.'

'Play *The Monday March Away*,' Jonathan said. 'Daresay the whole town's heard the rumours by now. We may as well announce it openly.'

Dressing in her bedroom, with the window on the latch, Susannah heard and recognized the tune. The words ran in her head:

> *Our rout came on the Thursday,*
> *on the Monday we marched away.*

The drums and fifes and bugles
so sweetily did play.
Some hearts they were merry,
but mine was full of woe.
She says: 'May I go along with you?'
'Oh no, my love, oh no.'

'I'll go down in some nunnery
and there I'll end my life.
I'll never have no lover now,
nor yet become a wife.
But constant and true-hearted, love,
for ever I'll remain,
And I never will get married till
my soldier comes again.'

8

Over the Hills and O'er the Main

Jonathan was gone, and there was no hope of hearing from him for several days. Abram spent the whole day at the bakery, and most of the night as well, and Pru served the customers with hardly a word. The apprentices were quiet as mice – no larking in the yard, no whistling in the bakehouse; even Billy was as sober as a sexton.

On the third day Susannah came home from school, tired out from pretending not to hear the whispers, and found that Banker Pratt's wife and sister were drinking tea with her mother in the parlour – 'And plying her with questions about your sister,' Harriet told her. 'Her true friends have better sense. You won't find Mrs Tree or Mrs Verney fishing for scandal with the sugar tongs.'

Susannah felt she could not face the Pratt ladies, but nor could she hide from them in the kitchen, so she went across the yard to seek refuge in the bakehouse. Abram was there, and Col, and to her surprise all three apprentices. 'A special order, Sukey love, there's a grand dinner planned tomorrow night aboard the flagship, and the commodore wants them fancy Portugal cakes your Da sometimes bakes for Myngs, and chestnut cream tartlets besides. I don't have the recipes and couldn't read them if I had. Can you look in your Da's daybook?'

Susannah fetched the daybook from the office. It was a massive leather-bound book which lived in its own stout Bible box, and in it, every evening, Jonathan noted down

49

each day's bakings, recorded his recipes, and wrote up any event important to Olivers', such as the taking on of a new apprentice. As Susannah turned the pages, she came upon the recipe for the cradle cake Jonathan had baked when she was born, the kichel cake Grandfather Oliver had baked for Polly's christening, the great wheatsheaf loaf to mark the end of Jonathan's apprenticeship as a baker, the sweetmeat pies that had been his 'master' piece as a pastrycook.

Josh came across the passage from the pantry where he had been mixing puff paste. 'Found the recipes, Miss Sukey?' he asked, wiping his hands on his apron.

'Oh, I'm sorry, Josh. I'm still looking – Yes, here, *Chestnut cream tartlets, Mr Lemarchand's recipe.* Da must have got this from that Frenchman, the émigré gentleman who died a year or so back.'

Abram trusted no Frenchman, whether émigré or open enemy; he said, 'Do the best you can, Josh lad, but us won't hold it against you if it don't turn out right.'

Josh grinned. He listened carefully as Susannah read out the recipe, repeated it back to her, and went off to make a start.

The Portugal cakes, though, proved elusive. Abram said, 'Seems a pity the British fleet can't order decent British baking. Shrewsbury cakes. Banbury cakes. They could do a lot worse than eat good Chelsea buns. And no need to go chasing uphill 'n down dale for a written recipe.'

'Portugal cakes,' Susannah said thankfully. 'Here it is. Flour, sugar, butter. Rose water, sherry wine. Eggs and currants.' She read out the instructions. 'Abram,' she said, 'do you think the Commodore's ordered them because the squadron's sailing for Lisbon?'

'That's the word along the Hard,' Abram said. 'Now, Sukey, don't you fret yourself. Likely your Da will catch up with your sister before ever she sets foot aboard the Lisbon packet. He'll fetch her safe home, you'll see.'

But Jonathan wrote from Falmouth saying the Lisbon packet had left port the day before he arrived in town. It had been crowded with officers' wives, their children and their servants, going to the war. He had booked a passage on the next sailing, and was certain he would trace Polly easily. His dears must not worry.

Mrs Oliver sent Martha out for a sea-chest and busied herself packing his clothes for the voyage. Being occupied did her good. 'He'll need food,' she said, 'food for the voyage. Harriet, send Martha round to the butcher's, and bid her tell Mr Bullus I want his best beef – enough for a big pot of beef cheese, and portable soup besides – and bacon likewise, and his best suet.'

While her mother and Martha minced beef and bacon and suet for the beef cheese, Susannah stewed beef bones for the portable soup, skimmed the broth, and poured it into thimble pots to set. It was sticky, messy work, and cleaning the stewpot was stickier and messier yet. She spread a flannel cloth on the bakehouse table and turned out the pots. The little chunks of meat jelly would dry out overnight in the bakehouse heat, and come morning be firm enough to pack.

When she went upstairs to bed, her parents' door was open and she glanced in to see her mother kneeling by the dower chests. Year by year, since Polly was born, Mrs Oliver had added to the stock of household linen kept in the dower chests: two tablecloths, a pair of blankets, pillow slips and sheets and towels, all safely stored against the wedding day. Susannah slipped past and went upstairs to her own room.

Cassy called next morning, bringing a little bundle of gifts for Polly, and a parcel wrapped in brown paper. 'We wondered if you might find room for these,' she said. 'Just in case. We wouldn't want Polly to feel friendless if – There's a handkerchief from me, and a thimble from Fanny Challen, lace bobbins from the Verney girls – all small things except – well, Barbary's parcel. She's . . . on friendly terms with several of the soldiers at the garrison, you see, and it seems one of them told her that out in the Peninsula the Army's been issued with great iron kettles that take an hour or more to boil, even on a sackful of wood. She says that with a light tin kettle to boil in a trice on a handful of twigs, Polly will be the most popular wife in camp.' She hesitated. 'Barbary believes that Polly will reach the lines, you see. That she will find Dick. I – I hope she is right. We all hope that she is right.'

Susannah's uncles sent a waggonload of grain from their farm, and Will hoisted it safely up into the grain-store. Abram watched with relief. 'The Lord be thanked for his mercies,' he said, '*that* should see us safe through the autumn, and Harvest Supper besides. Joshua, you'd best send two sacks down to the Mill come the morrow, flour bin's running low. Billy 'n Sam can make a start on bolting the flour come Wednesday – every speck of it's precious, don't you let them forget that. And see to it they don't waste the bran neither. Daresay we're in for another lean winter, with the price of wheat going up from day to day. Still, Harvest Supper first – can't skimp on that. What'll us bake for the harvest breads, Sukey love?'

Mrs Oliver came in and overheard his last words. 'Harvest breads?' she repeated, as if she could not remember what the words meant.

'For the Mayor's Supper, Mam, in the Market Place,' Susannah said. 'Da bakes for it every year.'

'Your father's at sea.'

Susannah glanced at Abram. 'Yes,' she said. 'We were trying to decide what to bake.'

'He won't be home in time.'

'Yes, but – we need this order, Mam. Da'd say so.'

52

'I see. Yes, I see.' Mrs Oliver went away, and Susannah sighed.

'Apple bread last year,' Abram said, thinking back. 'Spiced plum the year afore.'

'Pear bread, then?' Susannah said hesitantly.

'Aye, that might fit. There's a barrel a' pears your Da candied last autumn. Pear breads, then, with a dash a' perry in the dough, and cinnamon to spice it. Revel buns, a' course, gingerbread, the wheatsheaf. Naught there to fret over.'

Harvest Supper was open to all comers, each household bringing a pie, or a cheese, or a jug of ale. The Mayor provided the harvest breads, and every year Jonathan made his Master Baker's 'piece' over again, a great peck loaf shaped like a sheaf of wheat and glinting like the living grain in the fields. This year, though, it was Abram who made it, while the apprentices baked buns and gingerbread, and one and all helped with the harvest loaves. Will and the boys dragged the loaded cart down to the Market Place, where trestle tables had been set up and Pru, Harriet and Martha were helping to set out the platters. As she wrote up the daybook, Susannah could hear people hurrying down the street to get their places. The fiddlers struck up *Harvesters' Garland*. The yard was quiet and full of shadows, and the kitchen window unlit. Her mother must be alone in the parlour. She sighed, and wrote her name at the foot of the entry, closed the book and put it away safely; and then, unable to put it off longer, got up and went to join her.

A dozen pupils, most of them older than Susannah, attended the little school in Miss Honeywood's parlour. One afternoon, soon after the Harvest Supper, when the other girls had been whispering and wondering about Polly almost all day, and Miss Honeywood herself was talking, low-voiced, to her elderly maid and shaking her head sadly,

Susannah decided she could bear it no longer. She looked Miss Honeywood in the eye and said she was not feeling quite herself, and was given leave to go home early. But she did not want to go home either, to a mother brooding over Polly, to a troubled Abram and a tight-lipped Pru. Instead she walked along the walls, past the prim cottages of St Nicholas, past the Sea Gate, past the crowded rookery of St Andrew's, to where the old mast stood sentinel at the end of the great West Rampart, a seamark to ships coming home. Gulls were crying round the masthead and wheeling away across the graveyard, where a girl with a trowel and a basket was tending one of the newer graves. Susannah recognized Cassy and turned away, not wanting to disturb her. She walked to the end of the rampart where half a dozen steps led down to a sentry's nook, overlooking the sea. Someone was there before her: Barbary Chance, perching on the wall with one shoe swinging from her toe, unconcerned at showing off her ankles. The white thread stockings she was wearing were as respectable as Susannah's own, but she had painted the heels of her shoes coral-red.

'Playing truant from Miss Acidity's parlour?' she said, raising her eyebrows. 'That deserves a reward. Here –' She took a sugar-paper poke out of her pocket and tipped three candied plums into Susannah's hand. 'The best your cousin has in stock. No, don't fret, I promise there's no need – your Cousin Henniker's safe from me, he likes his snug, respectable life, poor man, and has sense enough to know it. The nearest he'll ever come to tossing his cap over the windmill is moping after your Polly, and it's my belief he only did that because he knew her heart was already bespoke. No, one of the silk-weavers bought me these, hoping I'd tell Madam Scritchscratch his ribbons were the best she could buy and just what I needed to trim next spring's bonnets. What tale did you tell Miss Acidity?'

'I said I wasn't feeling well,' Susannah admitted, 'but we

54

both knew it wasn't true.'

'I ought to march you back there,' Barbary said lazily. 'I should like to see her face if I did. She'd be burning angelica root all night long to purify her parlour.'

'You're playing truant yourself, from the workroom,' Susannah pointed out.

'No such thing – take some more plums, do. Madam H. gave me leave of absence to visit my poor Da's grave.'

'But I thought –'

'That I'm a foundling? And so I am. And often give thanks for it, when I see someone like your Polly hedged about with what she owes her parents. "How could you treat your poor mother so?"' she quoted cheerfully. '"You'll bring your poor father's grey hairs in sorrow to the grave." No, I'm spared all that, praise be. But now and then I want an hour away from the workroom, and if Madam H. gave me leave to go what would she do about the other girls, and all the other apprentice milliners up and down Bugle Street? So we agreed between us, with never a word spoken out of place, that from time to time I could take an hour or so to walk by the grave of my long-lost father. I picked one out for him,' she said, 'one of the drowned men's graves by the wall – sheltered, you see, he's really very fortunate – and once a month, or thereabouts, I play the dutiful daughter. Does it suit me?'

Susannah laughed. 'To admiration,' she said.

'That's just your Polly's choice of words,' Barbary remarked. 'When we were small, some of the other girls were spiteful little cats – *Barbary Ellen, Barbary wild, Dumped on a doorstep, Chance's child,*' she sang in the clear sweet voice that had once made her undisputed leader of a gang of children singing for pennies in the streets. 'Don't look so surprised, Susannah, did you suppose I didn't know? And some of them were kind, or tried to be – would I like to play hopscotch? or have a bite of barley sugar? But your Polly did neither of those things, and I always liked her the better for it. Cassy Woodling, now – She can't help her sweetness, but it sticks fast in my throat. Did you see her, down in the graveyard? She's got a basket of shells she gathered on the Eastcliff shore and scrubbed clean to border her man's grave. *She'll* never need to make believe she mourns.'

She set out the plum stones in a pattern on the rampart and flicked them away with her finger-nail: '*One she mourned, two she scorned, three she cast away. Four she wrecked, five she checked, six she teased to stay. Seven she missed, eight she kissed, nine the man that tarried. Ten she dropped, eleven she mocked, twelve the man she married.* What are you thinking, behind that solemn face?'

'Remembering how Polly and I counted plum stones in the kitchen, a few nights before Dick marched away,' Susannah said. 'And she had eight, right enough – eight for a soldier. If Mam had been there, she'd have slipped a couple more on to Polly's plate – *Marry a collier, never go cold, Marry a banker, purse full of gold.*'

'Your Polly never cared for Banker Pratt's tongue-tied nephew,' Barbary said, 'and never pretended to, neither. There was just one thing she wanted from him, she made no bones about it. Information.'

'Information?' Susannah repeated, frowning.

Barbary's eyes glinted. 'You heard me right, Susannah Oliver.'

Susannah watched Barbary's red-heeled shoes swinging against the rampart, and wondered what she had meant. But given the chance to tease, Barbary would never tell.

Susannah said in a rush, 'Da loves Polly, plain as print, you need only look at what he's doing to find her – quitting the bakery, hurrying down to Falmouth, taking the ship to Portugal –'

'Yes, Baker's always struck me as the kind of man that dives headlong to the rescue and only then realizes it might have been more sensible to take his boots off first.'

Susannah flushed, but went stubbornly on: 'And whatever you may say about hedging, taking care is Mam's way of loving.'

'Your Mam disapproves of me,' Barbary said, 'and she don't pretend otherwise. I can respect that, true enough. But instead of laying out Baker's money on yellow muslin and embroidered ribbons to divert your Polly's thoughts, she'd have done better to invest it in some means better suited to win her daughter's peace of mind. You're frowning at me, Susannah, as black as your high-nosed schoolmistress with her Bible clutched fast to her bosom.'

'I don't follow what you're saying,' Susannah said frankly.

'Well, don't addle your brains trying. Your Mam wouldn't care for that. She'd sooner you wore out your fingers stitching one of Miss Acidity's everlasting samplers. Stitchery's all very well,' Barbary said, 'and mine earns me my living, but there's more to it than making rows of knots on a bit of linen.'

She swung herself round and jumped down from the rampart. Susannah glimpsed the trails of pimpernel embroidered on her stockings, the small green leaves curling round her ankles and one scarlet flower peeping over the heel of each shoe.

'Polly had a pair of stockings like that,' she said. 'White thread stockings clocked with pimpernels – but the clocks were above the knee, of course.'

'Of course,' Barbary echoed, primming her face. 'Hold it for or against me, I see no sense in wasting good embroidery where only the washerwoman's likely to see it.'

'Dick Fletching bought a pair for Polly at the Mayday Fair,' Susannah said. 'Stockings embroidered with pimpernel because up on the Downs they call it Shepherd's Joy. And some flowers made of shells –'

She broke off, looking at Barbary, and Barbary looked quizzically back at her, beginning to smile.

'Polly was wearing those stockings the day she disappeared,' Susannah said slowly. 'Da asked me to look through her clothes to see what was missing, and they weren't there.'

'Quite right,' Barbary said. 'I took a liking to those pimpernel clocks, but I thought it would look more fetching if I worked a matching flower on each heel. I did it last Sunday.'

'Polly gave them to you?'

'She did, yes. She wouldn't turn to Cassy Woodling for help,' Barbary said, 'for fear of distressing her – though give Cassy her due, she'd never have refused. She didn't want to ask the Verney girls, or Kitty Osborne, or the miller's daughter, or any of the others whose families might start questioning and fretting. She wouldn't risk losing your Harriet a good place. But she knew I'd relish helping her – as indeed I did. And she knew it would never cross your mother's mind that her well-brought-up Polly would take me into her confidence. So now you know, Susannah. You look as if your candle had blown out on a dark night, with you at the top of the cellar stairs. Polly knew what she was doing, I promise you that.'

'How did she go?' Susannah asked.

'That would be telling. And if I choose not to say, Miss Susannah, how will you go about making me?'

'I can't.'

'Quite so. Well, as you admit that, I daresay I could – well, let's not say set your mind at rest . . . satisfy your curiosity. About mid morning Madam H. went sailing off to call on some clients on the Eastcliff, taking both the girls with her to carry the hat-boxes, and leaving her sister in charge of the shop. Well, Sister soon had her hands full with customers. Your Polly slipped in by way of the yard, and I took her up to my attic, easy as winking. She changed her clothes – and made me a present of her stockings, and her handkerchief besides – and I cut her hair for her –'

'Her hair?'

'Yes, well,' said Barbary, watching her with amusement, 'she could have tucked it up in her beaver hat, but her disguise would have been short-lived, don't you think? She went as a clerk, Susannah – a young clerk from a banking house, bound for Portugal with a bundle of confidential papers, very urgent, very important. Yes, I cut her hair – I gave her a fine mannish crop. And I'd altered her clothes for her, too: she'd bought herself a man's coat and breeches in Chichester, a couple of weeks earlier, but of course she could hardly try them on at the time, nor do the alterations at home.'

Susannah said, 'We went to Chichester market a month since. So she'd had it in mind for weeks on end. And yes, I remember her carrying a parcel on the way home.' Polly had sat in the carrier's cart with her hands folded over the brown-paper parcel in her lap, humming *Mary Ambree* as they trundled homeward:

When captains courageous whom death could not daunt
Did march to the siege of the city of Gaunt,
They mustered their soldiers by two and by three
And the foremost in battle was Mary Ambree.

When her bold sergeant major was slain in her sight
Who was her true lover, her joy and delight,
Because he was slain most treacherously,
Then vowed to revenge him his Mary Ambree.

She clothed herself swift from the top to the toe
In buff of the bravest most seemly to show,
A fair shirt of mail then next slipped on she:
Was not this a brave bonny lass, Mary Ambree –

'Oh, Polly love,' Susannah said. 'And she set out for London as a clerk, on the Chichester Stage?'

'Nothing of the kind,' Barbary said. 'She went aboard the flagship, the *Admiral Crawford*, three clear days before the squadron sailed. She reckoned that would give her time to settle into her part, and look less suspicious than a last-minute arrival. And besides, if the Navy did see through her disguise, there'd be time enough for them to put her ashore with a flea in her ear. She had money enough to pay her passage to Lisbon, and a good story to buttress it – the London banks are helping to fund the war (where she got *that* from, you may guess) and seems one way they use to smuggle gold to Lord Wellington is to send couriers disguised as women, with the sovereigns stitched into their bodices. So there she was, a sober young clerk, a true patriot, young enough and slight enough to pass as a female if need be, with vital information for His Lordship. She packed a gown and petticoats in her cloakbag, under the shirts and neckcloths, and soon as she was safe ashore in Lisbon she meant to change back into woman's clothes and find some way of getting to the British lines. She thought it might be easiest to claim she was maid to an officer's lady – struck down with sickness the moment they landed, and left behind to recover while her mistress went on to join her gallant husband. And myself, I'd put money on her reaching the regiment, given the good luck she deserves.'

'So her ticket on the Stage –'

'Was a blind, yes. I put on her grey cloak,' Barbary said, 'and the dowdiest bonnet I ever wore in my life, even counting the days I was a child at the charity school and dressed to match. It had a black veil – like peering through a cloud of coal dust. I claimed the seat your Polly had booked, and as soon as we reached the King's Head at Birkley Cross I slipped down from the coach and offered my place to a butter-woman who was trudging to Chichester market. "Bless your sweet face, my dear," she said, as if I were Cassy

Woodling herself. I threw the bonnet over a hedge, begged a lift in a farm waggon, and was back at Madam H's in time to be flat on my bed, with a rag soaked in vinegar draped across my poor aching head and all the blinds drawn, just as she came clucking up the stairs to see why the workroom was deserted and the bonnets untouched. So now you know, Susannah, and are you going to run to tell your Mam?'

'No,' Susannah said.

'You needn't hold back for my sake, Miss,' Barbary said, putting on a saintly look. 'Your Mam could make mischief for me, I don't doubt, but Madam knows my value in the workroom, and even if she turned me out of doors I daresay I could make my way.'

'Not for your sake at all,' Susannah said. 'Mam's in such an agony over Polly, she doesn't need any new troubles.'

Barbary said, 'Fairly spoken.' She shook out her skirts. 'I'd suggest we walked together as far as Green Street,' she said, with a glint of a smile, 'but sure as Fate all the old tabbies would hear of it, and shake their heads, and hiss to each other about Baker's *other* daughter getting into bad company.'

Challenged, Susannah said, 'I'm not as poor-spirited as that.' They walked across the graveyard and through the Laystow Gate into town. When they reached the alley that led from Green Street to Bugle Street, Barbary paused. 'Polly gave me one thing more,' she said, 'and it's put away safe in my workbox. The shell flowers her Dick bought for her at the Mayday Fair – she brought them with her that morning, and she said to me, "The proper bridesmaid's gift." You should have been her bridesmaid by rights, I know – you and Cassy, I daresay – but I trust you won't grudge them to me.'

She waved to Susannah and went off down the alley, her coral-red heels flashing over the cobbles and the small scarlet pimpernels nidnodding at her ankles.

9

Frost on the Down

On the second of November, All Souls Day, children were singing as they went 'souling' down Simnel Street, something Polly and Susannah had never been allowed to do ('No daughter of mine is going to beg for pennies'):

> *Soul Day! Soul!*
> *The streets are very dirty,*
> *Our shoes are very thin,*
> *Good master and good missus,*
> *Pray drop a penny in:*
> *An apple and a pear,*
> *A plum and a cherry,*
> *Any good thing*
> *To make us merry:*
> *One for Peter, two for Paul,*
> *Three for God who made us all –*
> *Soul Day! Soul!*

Susannah heard them as she sat in the bakehouse, trying to make sense of October's accounts. Abram had asked her to give an eye to the books while Jonathan was away. She found it easy enough to write out the bills and tot up the figures (Miss Honeywood's pupils did 'Household Accounts' twice a week), but deciding what the answers meant was far harder. She had been looking at last year's figures, to see how they compared. Bread, buns and gingerbread would keep Oliver's in credit, but the profits came from Jonathan's special bakings. Would he be home in time to bake for Christmas?

She went in search of her mother and found her polishing the parlour chairs with beeswax.

'I was wondering, Mam,' she began. 'Abram and the apprentices are going to be hard-pressed in the bakehouse. All the Christmas baking, you see –'

'Christmas?' Mrs Oliver said.

'Keeper cakes, Mam, and mincemeat, and Christmas loaves.'

Mrs Oliver said nothing.

Susannah swallowed. 'We could take on a journeyman, of course,' she said, 'but his wages would eat up any profit. If I helped, it would be another pair of hands, at least. But there's school.'

Mrs Oliver still did not answer, and after a moment or two Susannah went away. But at supper that night in the parlour her mother was cutting a slice of bacon pie into smaller and smaller pieces, and eating none of them; she said, 'I've written a note to Miss Honeywood, asking her to excuse you from school.'

Susannah was astonished. 'You've asked if she'd approve, Mam?'

'Of course she won't approve,' Mrs Oliver said tartly, sounding more like her old self. 'She'll lose the fees. But your father treasures the bakery, and I don't doubt he'd be pleased that you wanted to help.'

Abram welcomed the idea. He relied on Josh and Col, but he kept a watchful eye on the light-hearted Billy and worried about doing his duty by Sam. Susannah had had the freedom of the bakehouse since she was old enough to toddle across the yard, and she had picked up enough to make herself useful with the Christmas preparations. It made an agreeable change, too, from Miss Honeywood's parlour.

For a full week the bakery was given over to making

mincemeat. Pru and Harriet and Martha were pressed into service to chop apples and peel, to stone raisins, to squeeze lemons, to shred George Bullus's best suet, to pound and sieve Cousin Henniker's massive sugar loaves. And when the mincemeat was made, and the stoneware jars sealed with the Oliver trademark and ranged on the storeroom shelf, it was time to start work on the keeper cakes.

A letter came at last from Jonathan in Lisbon, saying that though he had not yet traced Polly, his dears must not lose heart. He was sure he would have better news when next he wrote.

Susannah told Abram, who said, 'Pray the good Lord he's right. How's your Mam taking it?'

'With hardly a word.'

'Ah well,' Abram said, 'each to his own way. Mince-meat's ripening just as it ought, and that's as well with Clement 'n Catherine coming up fast.'

St Clement's Day was the twenty-third of November. He was the patron saint of seamen and blacksmiths, and every year the ships' chandlers and the ironmongers ordered baskets of Clementy cakes to give to their customers in honour of his feast. Susannah fetched out the anchor and the horseshoe moulds. On St Clement's morning the bakery smelled spicy and sweet. Old Will twisted ribbons and ivy round the horseshoe nailed above the shop door. At midday, with a flash and bang of gunpowder, the smiths fired their anvils in salute, filling Westgate Street with puffs of acrid smoke, and from the harbour far below the seamen answered with musket fire.

St Catherine's Day, the twenty-fifth, was quieter. She was the patron of lacemakers, wheelwrights and unmarried girls. The carters twined coloured streamers round their wheelspokes and wore knots of ribbon on their whips, and there was a Lace Fair in the Market Place. The bakery sold Catherine-wheel cakes – large open mincemeat tarts, with rim and hub and spokes of pastry – and every unmarried girl in town ate a slice for luck. As she crumbled her piece, Susannah remembered her father at the kitchen table last November, cutting fat slices for herself and Polly, Harriet and Martha, and saying, as he did every year, 'Time to start the plum puddings.'

Abram had been thinking the same. The following day he mixed the Christmas puddings and tied them up in linen cloths: one for each of the boys, one for Harriet and one for Martha, a big one for the household, and five to spare. Col laid and lit a fire on the bakehouse hearth, hung the big iron pot over it, and trudged to and fro with buckets of well-water. The puddings bobbed in the pot like outsize dumplings. 'Plum pudden!' Col said, sniffing the smell of hot wet linen and rich spicy mixture. 'Best bit a' Christmas!'

'Beef's best,' Sam argued. 'Ribs a' Christmas beef!'

'You get on with your work, or it'll be bread-'n-pull-it all round,' Abram said. He ticked off the list of Christmas baking on his fingers so that Susannah could check the stores. 'Biscuits and gingerbread for the Eve, Sukey love. Christmas pies and Christmas loaves on the Day. There's almond paste to make, a week or so afore, and if us can manage it, some of those fancy Italian meringues your Da makes – they'd go down well at the evening parties.'

Mrs Oliver and Pru and the maids spent the week before Christmas sweeping and scrubbing. They cleaned the pewter and copper and brass, washed and ironed all the linen, scrubbed the bakeshop shelves, polished the floors. Col and Sam fetched the Yule log and a great heap of holly and ivy from the woods across the river. Susannah made Christmas garlands for the shop and the parlour, and old Will fastened bunches of holly to the front door, the shop door, the dole door and the yard gate.

On Christmas Day Susannah woke early to hear the church clock chime four. Her mother was already up and dressed, and busy in the kitchen, with Harriet singing as she stuffed the turkey and Martha scurrying like a mouse between two brisk cats. Susannah ran across the yard to the bakehouse, where Abram was glad to see her. 'Merry Christmas, Sukey love. We're sadly behind without your Da, but pastry's made and waiting – reckon you and Sam could cope with the Christmas pies?'

Susannah rolled out the pastry on the marble slab in the pantry and Sam set to work with the oblong cutters. 'Josh says we should get a hundred out of this batch,' she told him. 'Flip the sides up, pinch the corners, put in a spoonful of mincemeat – see? Cover it with the lid, crimp them together, make a hole to let the steam out, and it's ready to be glazed and baked. Only ninety-nine to go.'

It took them twice as long as it should have done. Susannah remembered watching her father – quick, deft, humming a carol as he worked. The ovens would be cooling – and that meant soggy pies, undercooked pastry. There was no sense in fretting, though: they could only do their best. She set her teeth and worked on. The pies were ready at last – some misshapen, some collapsing, but Billy and Col carried them off to be baked, and they came out of the ovens, row upon row of crisp brown mangers, oozing sweetness. As she and Sam dropped almond-paste stars on the glistening lids, the children crowding round the street window were singing:

> Dame get up and BAKE your pies,
> Bake your pies, bake your pies,
> Dame get up and BAKE your pies,
> It's Christmas Day in the morning.

Billy and Col were carrying trays of spicy Christmas loaves into the shop, where plum cakes, gingerbreads and fresh brown cobs were already stacked high on the shelves.

Josh set-in the last batch of breakfast rolls. The delivery boys sat down to clear a plateful of Christmas pies while the baskets were filled.

'What's to pipe, sir?' Tom asked Abram.

'*God Rest You Merry Gentlemen*, lad – what else?'

Susannah handed out the dole, giving a Christmas pie to any child, and then helped Pru in the shop until it was time to walk down Simnel Street to church. There had been small chance to miss Jonathan and grieve over Polly until now, but once she was settled in the pew beside her mother, she thought of little else. After church, Martha set off along the river to her home, lugging a basket of plum cake and Christmas pies, but Abram and Pru, Harriet and old Will, joined Mrs Oliver and Susannah for Christmas dinner in the kitchen. Harriet dished up the turkey 'alderman-style', in a coat of frizzled brown breadcrumbs with a chain of sausages across its breast – 'Mr Mayor should look half so fine,' old Will remarked. Abram asked the blessing and carved the bird. The Yule log crumbled on the hearth, the pudding bounced merrily in the pot above it, the kitchen was full of good savoury smells, but the company was subdued, remembering other years, and when the meal was over, the Trowers excused themselves, Harriet hurried away to see her sister (a housemaid in one of the Eastcliff villas), old Will gave his cats a Christmas dinner of their own – turkey giblets and yesterday's herring – and stumped away to his favourite alehouse; Susannah and her mother sat in the silent parlour, with Polly's ghost between them.

The January mornings were black and cold. 'Freeze-pot weather,' Harriet said as she stirred the porridge over the kitchen fire. 'Take my advice, Susannah, and get a good dose of Mr Woodling's peppermint mixture inside you before you go running across that yard. And mind you put your cloak on. Your Mam frets.'

'Not because she's afraid I'll catch cold,' Susannah said. 'She thinks she'll never get me back in Miss Honeywood's parlour with my sampler on my knee.'

'This time a' year there's a lot to be said for working in a bakehouse,' Harriet said, 'but from April to October I'm on your Mam's side. She's eating her heart out for word from the Peninsula.'

'Oh Harriet, I know. Surely we'll hear by the end of the month.'

But the days crawled past and there was no word. At the end of January, Susannah fetched out the daybook to remind herself of February's special bakings. Candlemas on the second of February: her grandfather had baked kichel cakes for Candlemas, year after year. *Kichel cakes, small size*, she read; and again, *Godchildren's cakes (kichels)*. She read it out to Abram. 'I'd forgot that,' he said, 'but it's true enough. You know them big kichel cakes your Da bakes for christenings? Well, come Candlemas your granddad allus baked little plum cakes – the same recipe – just big enough to sit on a child's hand, and people bought them for their godchildren, like giving a blessing.'

'Why at Candlemas, especially?'

Abram shook his head at her. 'That's no question for a Christian to ask,' he said. 'Candlemas Day, the Virgin Mary took our Saviour to the Temple in Jerusalem, and he was blessed and given his name, like a baby at its christening.'

'Would people in town – customers, I mean – remember?'

'Don't see why not,' Abram said. 'I'll get Pru to spread the word a bit. Write 'em down, Sukey love, and we'll try it.'

Susannah wrote it on the slate: *Candlemas, little kichel cakes*. On St Valentine's Eve there was to be a lavish wedding party for Joseph Gooding's daughter Louisa. Gilded gingerbreads and queen cakes for St Valentine's Day itself. Lardy cakes and apple tarts for the choirboys' supper on Shrove Tuesday. And then, praise be, came Ash

Wednesday and the beginning of Lent, and though there would still be special orders for christenings and funerals, and Lent buns scattered with caraway seeds to mark the spring sowing, there would be no more wedding breakfasts, no more parties, until Easter, six weeks later – and by then, surely, Jonathan must be home.

On Candlemas Day people took down their Christmas garlands. Holly and ivy, tinder-dry, burned fiercely on the kitchen fire. Gipsies came into town to sell bunches of snowdrops at the street corners. Jonathan called Candlemas 'the year's bakestone' – the day when, with Christmas behind them, people looked towards the promise of warmer spring weather and the long days of summer. Susannah sucked her sore fingers: she had spent most of the previous day rubbing seeds out of the raisins for the little kichel cakes, but at least Pru had reported that customers had snapped them up. Abram was worrying about Louisa Gooding's wedding. Her father was one of the most prosperous tradesmen in town and meant to turn his daughter out in style, and Louisa herself wanted to dazzle her country cousins with almond cakes, chocolate pies, and the famous Italian meringues which Susannah heartily wished her father had never made. Largest of all loomed the bride-cake, which must be baked, smoothly coated with almond paste, and lavishly adorned with sugar icing.

The wedding breakfast was ready at last. The first batch of chocolate pie-crust proved so brittle that Josh had to make it over again, a dozen almond cakes scorched and were sold off in the shop at a reduced price; but the meringues turned out perfectly, and the cake was both rich and handsome. Abram had told Billy he could choose and bake the wedding favours – 'None of your jokes, mind, pick summat that'll please the bride.' Billy grinned: 'A nice fat moneybag?' he suggested. 'Or a pair a' manacles?' But he came up trumps with dozens of gingerbread coach-and-horses (Louisa was

69

marrying a haulier), harness and wheels picked out with bright gilding.

Louisa's wedding waggon trundled up Simnel Street, carrying her and her bridegroom to their new home, as Susannah was busy with the agreeable task of writing out Joseph Gooding's bill, while Josh greased the heart-shaped patty pans ready for Valentine's Day. Children chased after the waggon, reaching for Billy's gingerbreads and singing as they went.

Susannah laughed as she listened. 'You used to go singing up and down the streets, didn't you, Josh? What was it like?'

'It's a good way of earning pennies or getting a bellyful of buns,' Josh said, thinking back. 'Just as soon as a baby was safe born and named, we'd be round the window singing – sixpence each, every time. Weddings were good too, and so was the King's Birthday, but there's nothing to touch a British victory. When word came of Trafalgar, and Admiral Nelson's death, we sang *Old Benbow* and *Hearts of Oak* all along Trumper Street, and it was a shower of shillings at every house. My Mam said the Admiral kept us in coals all that winter, and she blessed his name.'

'Who decides what they're going to sing?' Susannah asked, thinking of Barbary.

'Oh, there's allus one stands out as leader. Has a good ear for a tune, maybe, or can trim up a song to fit the folk concerned – times you can make more being paid to break off singing an apt bit of verse than ever you can singing for a homecoming or a new baby.'

'Yes, that I can believe,' Susannah said. 'I wonder what they'd have sung for Dick and Polly.'

Josh said, '*Lisbon Bound*, maybe, if he was a rifleman still. But if he'd turned to his own trade again, *O Shepherd*.'

From her bedroom that night Susannah looked across the yard to the glimmer of light from the bakehouse window.

70

Josh would doze through the night hours until the watchman knocked on the dole door to wake him, and Abram came hobbling along the alley. The moon was small but bright, the sky cloudless. There would be a sharp frost come morning. She climbed into bed, drawing back one curtain so that she should not sleep too late tomorrow, and the words of *O Shepherd* sang in her head:

> '*O shepherd O shepherd will you come home,*
> *Will you come home, will you come home,*
> *O shepherd O shepherd will you come home*
> *To your supper tonight?'*

> '*My sheep they are out on the frosty down,*
> *The frosty down, the frosty down,*
> *My sheep they are out on the frosty down,*
> *I cannot come home tonight –'*

Susannah pulled the featherbed up to her ears, but she could not shut out the thought of Polly and Dick and Jonathan out there in the dark, seeking one another in vain.

In the morning the shop was crowded with customers buying heart-shaped queen cakes and making a careful choice of gingerbread favours – gilded hearts, true-love knots, lovebirds. Mrs Oliver came into the shop to help Pru and Susannah. She was not at her best behind the counter – sharp with customers who didn't know their own minds, and apt to look down her nose at any comfortable gossip – but she stood no nonsense from the children, and she always gave the right change. Susannah made dozens of paper pokes, twirling each piece of blue sugar-paper into a cone, tucking the gingerbreads into it, and folding over the flap to keep all safe, while Pru counted the queen cakes carefully into customers' baskets, and Mrs Oliver dealt with the till. 'No word from your Polly, then?' one woman asked her; and another said, 'No news from Baker, poor dear man?' She did not answer – perhaps she truly did not hear.

At noon, when the shop was empty at last, Martha came scurrying in with three mugs of Harriet's pepperpot soup. A barrow man came up the street crying his wares. 'Sweet blue vi-lets! Come buy the spring's first vi-lets!' He stopped outside the shop, wedging the wheel with a stone. The shop bell tinkled as he came in carrying a small flower-pot with a clump of violets growing in it.

'Thank you, but no,' Mrs Oliver said firmly.

'For Baker's daughter, Missus,' the man said patiently. 'They be paid for – not a farthing due. I was down the Fort last spring, selling some pots a' Lent lilies to the Colonel's lady, and I got talking to a soldier lad that was reckoning to be shipped to Spain any day. And he paid me sixpence down, then 'n there, to bring a pot a' flowers to his girl come Valentine's.'

'That was kindly done,' Pru said, as Susannah bent to smell the sweetness of the flowers.

Mrs Oliver said nothing.

10

It Was on Easter Day

On Shrove Tuesday Harriet tossed pancakes in the kitchen for all comers, and the apprentices joined the riotous game of football which men and boys played up and down the streets, ward against ward, as long as breath and strength held out. Billy and Sam came to work on Ash Wednesday with skinned knuckles and bruised shins, but Col, who could run like a hare, was unmarked, and Josh had not only kept clear of the scrimmages himself but managed to fetch his brother Tom home unscathed as well.

In the slack cold days of Lent the town was quiet, drawing breath for spring. Susannah was helping Billy in the bolting-room one morning when they heard Col shouting up the stairs: 'Come quick, Miss Sukey! There's word of a great victory in Spain –' Still in her bolting-smock, spattered with flour from head to toe, she ran down to the Market Place; a crowd was swarming into The Egg's yard, and there, drawing all eyes, was the London Mail, with red ribbons streaming from the coachman's whip and laurels on its roof.

On an icy January night the British army had stormed the city of Ciudad Rodrigo, and won a mighty victory. The *Courant* brought out a special issue, and Susannah read every word. It was clear that Dick's regiment, the Ninety-Fifth, had been in the thick of the fighting. The British had captured a hundred and fifty guns and two thousand prisoners, the roads into Spain lay open, the army

73

was on the march. She thought of Dick – wounded, dying, killed? – and of Polly, heaven knew where. Neighbours and friends who came to ask after Jonathan hardly won a civil word from Mrs Oliver. Cousin Henniker came, and sighed, and shook his head, and took himself off again to Green Street, looking like Sexton at a funeral. 'I begin to think your sister was right about him,' Mrs Oliver said, to Susannah's surprise. 'A nice enough lad, but he belongs in the chimney corner. He wasn't made for wind and weather.'

Three days later Susannah came into the kitchen to find Harriet carving a plate of cold beef for a crippled soldier while Martha ran in and out bringing a feather pillow, the parlour footstool, a blanket to wrap round his shoulders. 'There, there, lass,' he was saying, 'I'm not ninety yet, thanking you kindly all the same. Sergeant Nicholls, Miss,' he said, catching sight of Susannah, 'invalided home from the war. I met your dad in Lisbon and he gave me a message for you. He's still looking and still hopeful, and sends his dear love to you and your Mam.'

The sergeant's thigh had been shattered and he would never walk straight again, but reckoned himself lucky to be alive, and in his wits, and safe ashore in England. They saw him off on the Portsmouth Stage with five shillings in his pocket and a bundle of bread and cold meat for his journey. Though his message told them nothing new, it did them good, and it was with a lighter heart that Susannah looked up the Mothering Sunday bakings recorded in the daybook. Some bakers sold wafers for Mothering Sunday, some fig cakes or 'lambs-tail' comfits, but Jonathan baked simnel cakes – 'Can't hardly do less,' he said, 'living where we do' – and Susannah saw from the daybook that last year he had baked three hundred and sold every one. There was no need to read the recipe aloud – Abram knew it by heart. She helped Sam and Billy to blanch and shred and grind the almonds, to sieve the sugar, to clean the currants and chop the peel, to bolt the flour and sift it through a fine tammy sieve, to rub in lard and butter and beat up eggs. When the first batch came out of the oven, they all paused, weary and sweating, to watch Abram break open one cake, sniff, taste and approve it, and share it out. It was light, sweet and spicy, and the taste of it meant spring.

Pru moulded dozens of simnel 'fancies' from almond paste: primroses, Lent lilies, cowslips – all the yellow flowers of spring. Sam and Billy stuck them to the cakes with dabs of honey, while Josh decked one large simnel with candied cowslips and violets from last year's store, to serve as centrepiece in the shop window.

By Sunday noon the bakehouse was empty, the shop locked and shuttered, the street deserted. All the maidservants in town, all the apprentices, all the young shopmen, had set off homeward for a day's holiday, with simnels tucked under their arms. Susannah's heart sank at the thought of an afternoon spent alone with her mother. She was frowning over the daybook, anxious not to let Abram down by running out of stores for the Easter bakings, when her mother came into the parlour.

'What are you doing, Susan?'

'Checking what we'll need for the Easter bakings, Mam,' Susannah said. 'Hot cross buns for Good Friday and solly cakes for Easter Day.'

Mrs Oliver said, 'I was thinking of going up to London, to spend a few days with your Aunt Soper.'

Susannah looked up in surprise. Mrs Soper, forceful widow of a London tobacconist, was Jonathan's only sister, but she and Mrs Oliver did not care for one another, and in twenty years had exchanged visits only twice. 'When will you go, Mam? And for how long?'

'On Wednesday, for a few days only. I'll be back inside a week. I don't suggest you come with me, Susan. I've enquiries to make, and calls to pay, and no doubt errands to run for half the town besides. There'll be small time to spare for seeing the sights, though I daresay your aunt would enjoy showing them off as if the entire city had been built to her directions.'

As soon as word of Mrs Oliver's plan got out, friends and neighbours came with commissions. Would she take a parcel to Henry Challen, serving his apprenticeship to a butcher in Southwark? Call at the Cross Keys in Holborn and see if young Lizzie Nye was well and happy? Discover what had become of the King's Creole snuff which Isaac Turner had ordered urgently, six weeks since, and for which he was still waiting? Harriet wanted a wedding handkerchief for her sister, Mrs Verney a christening gift for a godchild; and when Mrs Oliver called at Madam Henriette's to choose a bonnet for London, Barbary Chance put in a request for several yards of purl-edged ribbon. The bonnet was respectable but becoming, lined with silver-grey silk and trimmed with narrow crimson ribbon, and Susannah looked at it with interest.

Mrs Oliver left for London on the stagecoach with a list of commissions tucked into her glove, and Susannah expected her home five days later, at the start of Holy Week, but Maundy Thursday came and there was still no word from her. Abram was in the bakehouse on Thursday afternoon, mixing the dough for the following day. For once there would be no breakfast rolls, no bread, no cake; nothing but a thousand hot cross buns, each with a bold cross of almond paste on the shiny dark crust. Many families kept a hot cross bun in the kitchen all year round, for luck and blessing; it would dry out and harden, but never turn mouldy. Abram took down last year's from the bakehouse chimney-piece, and put the first of this year's baking in its place. Last year, and for twenty years before that, Jonathan had done the same. Wherever he was, whatever he was doing, his thoughts would surely turn to the bakery. But what about

Polly? When the children in the street sang 'One a penny, two a penny, hot cross buns', when the barrow men set a circle of green turves and white stones around the Market Cross, when the passing bell at St Nicholas tolled thirty-three times for the Saviour's death: each and every time Susannah wondered if Polly was remembering.

On the morning of Easter Saturday, Abram started work on the solly cakes for the following day. They were fashionable, expensive, and troublesome, needing the finest wheat flour, sieved through silk, and new milk warm from the cow. Billy set to work in the bolting-room, sifting the best flour through three tammy sieves, the first with a mesh of sixty, the second ninety, and the third a hundred and twenty holes to the inch. The dairymaid from Saltings Farm brought her best cow through the streets and milked her, then and there, in the yard. Col carried pails of warm foamy milk into the bakehouse, and the cats came streaming after him. 'Turn them creatures out, boy,' Abram said. He shouted up the stairs to Billy: 'Make haste, lad! You'll never set the tams afire at that rate.'

Jonathan liked to make his own yeast, using his father's recipe (a mixture of hops and potatoes), but to save time and trouble Abram had begun buying ale barm from Nye's Brewery. He sniffed the newest barm, which was brown and pungent; crumbled a scrap in his fingers; and thought it over. 'Reckon not,' he said. 'Fetch up last Wednesday's, Sam. It'll take longer to work, but the flavour's milder – better suited to the best wheat flour.'

The solly-cake dough was left to rise in the bakehouse all day long. The dairymaid brought back the cow that evening, milked her again, and promised to deliver cream on Easter morning. Susannah helped to mix more flour, salt and sugar, and the new milk into a thick paste ready for kneading. She scooped up a handful of the fine wheat flour and let it run through her fingers. It was creamy white,

77

dappled with bran and flecked gold from the wheat kernels. White and golden brown and cream, she thought, as Josh showed her how to fold in the starter dough: Easter's colours.

When she went upstairs to bed that night, on impulse she turned the handle of Polly's room. The air was cold and musty. She opened the window. Polly's room looked south-west, towards the shipyards and the sea. Susannah watched a lantern bobbing along Green Street: Sexton, going to unbolt the Laystow Gate so that the graveyard would stand open all Easter Night. She thought of Will Downer and Cassy, and then of Polly and Dick.

> *O shepherd O shepherd will you come home,*
> *Will you come home, will you come home,*
> *O shepherd O shepherd will you come home*
> *To your lodging tonight?*

Susannah shivered. She latched the window tightly. Her sleep was troubled by dreams of Polly, and she woke in the blowy dark before dawn. In the bakehouse the keelers were full of solly-cake dough, fragrant and alive. She helped to shape it into small rounds which were set to rise on the baking sheets. Sam was trying to copy Josh who could roll two at a time, one in each hand, expertly. The delivery boys arrived early, ready to sell hot cakes from door to door in time for breakfast.

As soon as the cakes came out of the ovens, light and crisp, pale as ivory, Josh brushed them over with egg-yolk glaze, and it set deep gold in the warmth of the fresh-baked dough. The boys began to wrap them in the linen cloths and stow them in the baskets. Solly cakes were a West Country speciality, split open, spread with clotted cream, and eaten hot. Jonathan's émigré friend, Mr Lemarchand, had told him that 'solly' was a French name, *soleil lune*, meaning 'sun

78

and moon', and as Susannah helped to pack them, this Easter morning, she saw why. 'The yellow sun above and the white moon below,' she said to Abram, pleased.

Abram grunted. 'Sounds like a good sturdy English name to me,' he said stubbornly. 'Thought your Da got the recipe from that cousin a' yours, down in Bath?'

'So he did, but – Oh well,' Susannah said. 'It doesn't matter. I only meant the carol fits the cakes.'

The boys went down Simnel Street with the baskets on their heads, Tom Herring blowing blithely on his pipe:

> *It was on Easter Day,*
> *And all in the morning,*
> *Our Saviour arose,*
> *Our own heavenly king:*
> *The sun and the moon*
> *They did both rise with him:*
> *And sweet Jesus we call him by name.*

11

The King's Birthday

Mrs Oliver returned three days later. When Susannah saw her, she stopped short in surprise. Her mother looked and sounded different: she moved briskly, there was colour in her face, her voice and her eyes were alive. 'Well, Susan, your aunt sends you her love, though she'll be sadly disappointed that you didn't run off with a tinker the moment my back was turned. Is Abram in the bakehouse? Good. There's a special baking to be put in hand as soon as possible. Give me, say, half an hour to unpack my bag, and I'll explain what I want.'

Within the half-hour they were waiting in the bakehouse: Abram, the three apprentices, Col and Susannah. Old Will was testing the grain hoist, in earshot of the bakehouse door, and Martha was loitering hopefully by the well, bucket in hand.

'Now,' Mrs Oliver said, 'a special baking of plum cake. The bride-cake recipe.'

Abram said, 'Spring's not the best time a' year for selling plum cake, Missus.'

'These cakes won't be for sale,' Mrs Oliver said.

'For what then, Mam?' Susannah asked.

'The Army, Susan. The Ninety-Fifth Regiment. I couldn't get a precise figure in London, but allowing for thefts and losses along the way, twelve hundred cakes should suffice – what your father calls single-size, I believe. Plus another four of the largest size, one each for the King, the Prince

Regent and the Duke of York here at home, and one for Lord Wellington out in the Peninsula. Your Aunt Soper will deliver the Royal cakes – and God save the King in sober earnest if she claps eyes on him, she'll back him into a corner and tell him how to run the country, and probably dose him with rhubarb pills into the bargain – and I'll ask Mr Tree's advice about shipping the rest to Portugal.'

'Shipping?' Susannah echoed.

'We shall have to hire a trading vessel, of course – don't hover there, Will, come in and listen at your ease. The Commissary's clerks in London will see to the paperwork if Aunt Soper keeps after them, *which* she will. There's a dozen transports sailing to Portugal next month with horses and arms and supplies, so if I hire a sloop for the cakes, it can join the convoy.'

'Missus, you'll never find a crew,' old Will said. 'There's not a man in fifty miles would set foot aboard, for mortal fear a' being pressed by the Navy.'

'I've been considering that,' Mrs Oliver said. 'There must be a dozen good seamen down on the Hard every day of the year – men unfit for sea service because they've lost a leg or been blinded in one eye. Offer them five pounds a-piece to make a single voyage to Portugal, and I dare swear they'd jump at the chance. Isn't that so?'

Old Will said, 'Maybe. Aye.'

Susannah said, 'Mam, who's to pay for all this?'

'This is a gift from Olivers' to the Ninety-Fifth. Don't look so anxious, Susan. We shall manage. And there's no time to waste. It wasn't easy to get permission from the Commissary and the Admiralty, and I don't want to give them time to think better of it. These cakes are a gift to the riflemen to celebrate the King's Birthday on the fourth of June – that's the tale I told in London, and we must hold to it.'

Abram said, 'What about a good basic plum-cake recipe, then? It'd save a deal a' trouble. Good plum cake, mind, moist 'n sweet.'

'No,' Mrs Oliver said. 'The bride-cake recipe. Wrapped and sealed with the bakery's trademark, and shipped off to Lisbon. The Commissary there dispatches them by waggon to the Army lines, and God willing they reach the Ninety-Fifth in due time.'

Susannah said persuasively, 'Listen, Mam. A good plum cake costs half as much as a bride-cake. And if – when – Dick Fletching gets his share – well, he'd be as like to recognize the mark on a plum cake as on a full-iced bride-cake, and Polly still more so.'

'No, Susan. Whether or not one of these cakes reaches your sister, I mean to send proper bride-cake, the sort that would have stood on the table at her wedding breakfast – the sort I would have handed to her as she sat in the wedding waggon. I doubt,' she said, 'that there's much chance she'll never go hungry, but if this message reaches her safely, she'll understand that it means a blessing. So list what we'll need for twelve hundred cakes, and work out what it will cost. And if there are no other questions' – she stood up, tying the crimson ribbons of her new bonnet – 'I'll call on Mr Tree.'

Old Will shook his head and went off, muttering, to the woodshed. Abram said, 'Well, we've had our orders, plain as day. Sukey love, reckon us had better have a word about what's to buy. Josh, fetch out the cake hoops. And as for you three' – he looked at Billy and Sam and Col – 'sit quiet and listen hard.'

Josh brought out the cake hoops. 'When the Master bakes his single-size keeper cakes, it's the two-hand hoop he uses,' he said, spanning the small hoop with his hands, thumb to thumb. 'We've a dozen a' these. For twelve hundred cakes, baking nine to a batch, and using all three ovens, us'd need to be baking night 'n day for weeks on end.

But there's the shop baking to do besides. Bride-cake needs to bake slow and steady. Reckoning two bakings a day, that'd be' – he paused, working it out on his fingers – 'four and a half dozen cakes. And we'd need more hoops.'

Abram looked at Susannah. 'Can you work out how many days, Sukey love?'

She reached for the slate and wrote down the figures. 'Twenty-four,' she said at last. 'That's allowing for the outsize cakes as well, but not for the almond paste or the sugar icing. I'll get the daybook.'

She found the recipe, copied into the daybook a few weeks before her grandfather's wedding day, and read it out.

'Four pounds of butter, two of sugar. Thirty-two eggs. Four pounds of flour, spiced with nutmeg and mace. Half a pint of brandy. Two pounds a-piece of currants and raisins, one of almonds, three of candied peel. And for the almond paste, a pound of almonds, a pound of sugar, the yolks of three eggs. And for the sugar icing, two pounds of sugar, a little cornstarch, the whites of five eggs. What size cake should that make, Abram?'

'A twenty-pounder, I reckon,' he said. 'It'd feed a hundred, easy. There's enough mixture there for, say, nine single-size hoops. Call it one batch.'

Susannah scribbled down the figures. 'Mam wants – what? – a hundred and thirty-three batches, and four outsize cakes as well, so if I multiply it by 140, we should be close enough.' She worked out the first sum, and swallowed hard. 'That means 560 pounds of butter in all, or about 24 pounds a day. Twenty sugar loaves. And – Lord above – 4,500 eggs.'

'What's that a day, Sukey?'

'Two hundred or thereabouts.'

'Praise be it's spring,' Abram said. 'And 560 pounds a' flour, I daresay? Well, us can manage that easy enough.'

Susannah said, 'But with grain the price it is, what will the town say?'

Billy said, 'On the King's Birthday some years since, the gentry a' Chichester raised a hundred pound to give the militia a grand dinner – beef and mutton and ham and strong beer for a thousand men. And not a word said against it.'

'Flour's different,' Susannah said. 'You may not eat beef from one year's end to the next, but without your daily bread you starve.'

Abram said, 'That's true enough, Sukey, but there's not a woman in this town wouldn't do the same for her own, and I reckon they'll say as much. What's next?'

Susannah looked back to her list. 'Nine gallons of brandy,' she said. Billy whistled softly. 'Currants and raisins, 280 pounds a-piece. Peel, 420, and almonds, 140. Or at a daily rate, say twelve, twelve, eighteen, six. And another 140 pounds of almonds, 420 pounds of sugar, and 700 eggs for the almond paste and the sugar icing.' In her mind's eye she saw a mountain of currants and raisins waiting to be cleaned, enough candied peel to pave the Market Place, enough almonds to tile the church roof.

'Cornstarch, mace, nutmeg, rose water,' Abram said.

'Paper, string, sealing wax,' added Josh.

Susannah said, 'It won't do, truly it won't. We must persuade Mam to let us bake one cake, just one, and despatch it to Dick.'

Abram said, 'Sukey love, *one* cake would be stolen before ever the ship set sail. A dozen, or a score, or a hundred, the same. But a cargo of twelve hundred cakes, sent by official permission, stamped with official seals, that's a different thing.'

'I suppose you're right,' she admitted. 'But the cost of it –'

'Ah, you must take that up with your Mam, love.'

When Mrs Oliver came home from calling on Christopher

Tree, Susannah was waiting for her in the parlour.

'What did Mr Tree say, Mam?'

'Poor man, he thought at first that fretting over your sister had unbalanced me altogether. But I showed him the letters of permission I got in London, and that eased his mind. He'll make some enquiries about hiring a ship and finding a crew, and if the Lord is kind we can sell off the ship when the voyage is done and set that against the costs. I called on Banker Pratt as well, and he will advance me £300.'

Susannah swallowed. 'Mam, that's four times the profit we'd make in a *good* year, and as things stand we're making far less.'

'I've put up the house as security. This house, Susan. Gentry folk mightn't care to hire a house overlooking a baker's yard, but it has its own front door and its own bit of garden, kitchen and parlour, master bedroom and closet, and two bedrooms above, and Mr Pratt thinks he should have no difficulty in finding a respectable merchant or tradesman to rent it. The house is your father's, of course, but Banker Pratt knows he will make my word good, so he is satisfied and we must make shift to be the same. There'll be a deal of sorting out and spring-cleaning to do for the tenants – they'll want the rooms furnished, of course – but Harriet and I can cope with that. Abram will need your help, I don't doubt.'

Susannah went away to the bakehouse, leaving her in the trimly furnished parlour which was her pride and joy.

Abram had mixed a tester batch of bride-cake; Col had fired 'King Harry'; Josh had greased and lined the cake hoop. The cake came out of the oven late that afternoon. A little of the mixture had, as usual, oozed between the hoop and the baking sheet on which it stood. These crisp sweet curls were one of Col's perks, and he scooped them up cheerfully.

'Tastes prime!' he said.

When the cake had cooled a little, Abram eased it out of the hoop and cut it up. It was still warm and crumbled in the mouth, spicy and sweet. The tinsmith called at the bakery in time to be offered a piece, praised it heartily, and agreed to supply a dozen single-sized hoops next day. Susannah walked down to Chartman's, where she astonished the shopman by buying two reams of paper and fifty sticks of sealing wax. When she returned, she found Col working out how many brushwood bundles they would need. He paced to and fro, from 'Daniel' to 'Queen Jane' to 'King Harry' and back again, counting the notches on his tally sticks. 'A dozen fifty times over, Miss Sukey,' he said at last. 'That's as about as many as us'd use in a month, baking every day. 'Tain't so easy to get fuel come spring. Reckon it'll cost all a' five pound.'

'You'd better get in what you can,' Susannah said. 'I doubt if my Mam will change her mind.'

12

Making Ready

Word of preparations for a grand baking at Oliver's ran
around the town. People watched with interest as Cousin
Henniker's porter heaved sack after sack of currants up
Simnel Street. 'Who's getting wed?' Susannah heard
women asking in the Market Place. 'There's been no banns
called in church.'

'There's another sugar loaf going up,' one woman said.
Sugar loaves were tall (half as high as a man), cone-shaped,
heavy and unmistakable. 'That makes fifteen so far. Maybe
Banker Pratt's giving a ball for that lanky daughter of his.'

'It'd show better sense if he laid out his money on rings for
her fingers.'

Susannah left them enjoying themselves and went on to
Bonallack's to order a firkin of brandy. 'Dear Lord, Miss
Susannah, that should drown a sea of sorrows.' When she
came back across the Market Place, the women were still
there and still speculating.

On market day Mrs Oliver went down the line of dairy
stalls, exchanging news and greetings with the farmers'
wives and explaining that Olivers' had a special baking in
hand and would need twenty-four pounds of fresh butter
and two hundred new-laid eggs delivered daily, Sundays
excepted, for the next four weeks. Could they oblige with,
say, two pounds of butter and two dozen eggs? Excellent.
From the coming Monday, then.

On the following day, Wednesday, Susannah sat by

herself in the pantry, surrounded by sugar loaves, slabs of candied peel, boxes of raisins, sacks of currants and almonds. She untied the nearest sack, scooped sticky black currants into her wire sieve, spread a cloth across her lap, and began work. Dust and grit sifted through the mesh. She shook out the cloth in the yard and began to rub the currants over the wire, picking out any bits of stalk and twig. Pru Trower came for a bowlful, to pick over when the shop was quiet; Martha came, and Mrs Oliver; when the daily baking was done, Abram sent the apprentices. Susannah's fingers grew sore, and when she closed her eyes to rest them, black dots jumped and scurried across the lids. The pantry overlooked Simnel Street, and the hum of the street was in her ears all day long. Horses clopped past, carts rumbled over the cobbles; street-sellers cried their wares above the barking of the dogs; women working at their doors called to one another, crooned over babies, exchanged the day's news. 'What's going on at Oliver's?' she heard them saying. 'Well, word is Baker's wife came back from London with a grand order.' At dusk the children whistled and sang as they ran past. They too had heard the rumours:

> The flour that makes this cake, sir,
> Would fill a hundred bins,
> The fire that bakes this cake, sir,
> Would roast the Devil's sins.

'They know we're dealing with a big order,' she told her mother that evening. 'But not what we're baking, or who it's for.'

'Word will get out soon enough,' Mrs Oliver said. 'No need for us to shout it through the streets.'

No daughter of mine shall be sung in the streets, Susannah thought, remembering how often her mother had said it.

'Banker Pratt called this morning,' Mrs Oliver went on. 'He thinks he may have found a suitable tenant. An elderly man – a retired schoolmaster – and the sister who keeps house for him.' She picked up the bowl of currants she was cleaning. 'Go to bed, Susan. You're looking tired.'

On the following day there was a knocking at the dole door. Susannah went to open it, half afraid she might find a hostile gathering – she had slept badly, dreaming of a faceless crowd smashing the pantry windows and shouting for bread – but there, all alone, stood Cassy Downer in her black-ribboned bonnet. Cassy said, 'Mr Henniker told Grandpa you had a plan, a special baking, something to help Polly.'

'Yes, but – well, it's Mam's idea, I ought to leave it to her to tell you –'

But Cassy put no questions. She said, 'If I could help, I would be very glad.'

They worked together, with hardly a word, for three hours, while other members of the household came and went, helping as and when they could. At midday Martha brought them a jug of buttermilk, a loaf and two plates of cold meat, and Mrs Oliver came in to thank Cassy. 'I'm glad to help,' Cassy said. She stayed all afternoon, and at the end of the day, unpinning her apron, said, 'I'll be back tomorrow, Sukey.'

'Oh Cassy, I'd be more than thankful.'

Cassy came back next day as the clock was striking eight and sat herself down with a sieve of currants. A few minutes later the Verney girls arrived, and soon after them Fanny Challen, Sally Bullus, Kitty Osborne. By noon there were a dozen girls at work, cleaning currants, stoning raisins, chopping candied peel. None of them asked outright about Polly, and Susannah hesitated to tell them the plan, partly because she felt it was her mother's place to do so, and partly because she dreaded putting it into words. Mrs Oliver joined the party soon after midday, bringing Harriet and Martha with her. The pantry was now so full that they moved to the bakehouse, where Josh and Sam were at work skinning the almonds.

Late that afternoon old Will showed Christopher Tree into the bakehouse. The shipbuilder looked around him in surprise. Mrs Oliver reached for a dishcloth to wipe the sticky currant juice off her hands and mop the beads and smears of blood where she had skinned her fingertips on the wire. She said, 'This is good of you, Christopher.'

'My dear Dorothy,' he said, 'surely you could hire a journeyman –'

'Thank you, but the girls are being wonderfully kind, and we cannot afford to spend the money on hired help.'

'Well now,' he said, 'I've some news of the commission you asked me to carry out. Would you sooner we went to the house?'

Mrs Oliver said, 'The news will be out fast enough, and I'd rather our friends here heard it first.'

'Right,' Christopher Tree said. 'Well, reckon I've found you a ship.' Susannah saw the girls glance at one another, and nod. 'I put the word out along the coast, and I'm told there's a sloop for sale at Chichester – older and leakier than I'd choose, but said to be sound. A good suit of sails but she'd need new rigging before she ventured Biscay. Young Kit and a couple of the lads will walk over to Chichester come Sunday, and if she fits the bill they'll sail her down, and we can see her safe-found and ready for sea. My foreman can see to the provisioning for you – pickled pork and hard biscuit and drinking water and ale. As to the crew,' he went on, 'I'm asking around, but that'll take a while longer. And if they sail her safe home again, which the good Lord grant they will, reckon you should be able to sell her again for a fair price. Name's *Constant Anne*, by the by.'

Mrs Oliver went with him to the yard gate. The bakehouse was quiet for a moment. Then Cassy said, 'Lisbon bound, Sukey?' and Susannah nodded.

'She hopes, Mam hopes, to – to get word somehow to Polly,' she said.

They got on with the work, and Fanny Challen began to sing softly:

> *I'll build my love a ship,*
> *A ship of noted fame,*
> *I'll have four-and-twenty seamen bold*
> *To box her on the main.*
> *They will rant and roar in sparkling glee*
> *Wheresoever they do go*
> *To the far far coast of Portugal*
> *To face the daring foe.*

Sam fetched the pipe and played as the other girls joined in:

> *There's not a lace goes round my waist*
> *Nor a comb goes in my hair,*
> *There's neither fire nor candlelight,*
> *Can ease my heart's despair,*
> *Nor neither will I married be*
> *Until the day I die*
> *Since the far far land of Portugal*
> *Did part my love and I.*

On Saturday they began the task Susannah had dreaded most: chopping up the sugar loaves and sifting them through a succession of sieves. When she went up to bed that night, after a day at the sugar-sifting, her right arm was too swollen for her to pull her sleeve over it – Harriet had to snip the cuff seam to rescue her. But neighbours called at the dole door offering help, and took away basins of chopped-up sugar to crush and sieve in their own kitchens, Abram put off the first cake-baking from Monday to Wednesday so that the apprentices could help, and Polly's friends were unfailing.

91

On Tuesday morning Susannah stole half an hour from the bakehouse and ran down Fore Street to climb the ramparts, hoping to see Kit Tree and his friends sailing into harbour that noon. There were several old boatmen on the ramparts, as there always were, watching the comings and goings in the harbour. They nodded to her, and one said, 'Reckon that's your Mam's just a-coming in – see? Needs new rigging but not a bad looker.'

Susannah craned over the ramparts. Shabby and down-at-heel as *Constant Anne* was, she looked fast – just as well since she would not be armed, and her only hope if the French caught sight of her was to out-sail them.

The rope-makers sent new cordage to the Hard, free of charge. Timothy Stenning, the town's Master Cooper and an old friend of Jonathan's, sent six new water-casks, sweet and clean, the best gift any crew could hope for. Solomon Nye, who owned the Brewery, offered six barrels of beer. Mr Tree picked a crew from a crowd of veteran seamen at the shipyard gates: a petty officer, crippled but tough as whipcord; a gunner's mate, blind in one eye and with a face blackened by gunpowder stains; a dozen sailors wounded in the wars; and to take command, a raw lieutenant, Mr Beamish, with no money and no family connections, who had been forced to resign from the Navy when he developed the sugar sickness, a disease which had no cure. Kit Tree called at the bakery with the news, and found the girls chopping the slabs of gummy candied peel. He sharpened the knives on the bakehouse doorstep and stayed all afternoon, helping as and where he could. 'First baking tomorrow, is it, Susannah?' he asked her. 'Good luck to all.'

When the helpers had gone at last, and the bakehouse was quiet, only Col and Billy still at work, struggling to force the brushwood bundles into the ovens in readiness for tomorrow's baking, Susannah stepped into the yard. It was tranquil there. She leaned against the wall for a moment and curled one arm behind her to ease the ache in her back. That was the way older women stood, shifting their weight from foot to foot. She felt as if she had aged ten years or more, and one of the songs that Jonathan sang as he bolted the new-milled flour hummed in her head:

> Out of the hopper like smoke she came
> And called the miller by his name:
> 'O miller,' said she, 'what shall I give thee
> To grind an old woman down young again?'

13

The First Baking

On the morning the baking began, Susannah joined Abram and Col and the apprentices in the bakehouse, leaving Polly's friends still hard at work cleaning and chopping and sifting. Billy and Sam had set out the cake hoops, the parchment, the knives and forks and spoons, the whisks and graters, the jugs and bowls, the pestle and mortar, and the scales: the table looked as if Jonathan might walk in at any moment, rolling up his shirt sleeves to begin the Christmas baking. There was a great heap of candied peel, chopped fine; a washtub brimming with almonds; a glittering mound of sugar. Old Will had driven his cart to the Downlands the day before, to fetch a cask of sweet clean water, straight from the spring, so that Sam could wash the currants and raisins, and spread them on flour sacks to dry overnight in the warmth of the bakehouse.

The dairywomen arrived, bringing blocks of freshly churned butter, each stamped with the mark of the farm where it was made – a trident for Saltings, kingcups for Meriden, a swan for Howick. The farmers' boys trooped into the yard bringing buckets of new-laid eggs.

'Now,' said Abram, 'you weigh out the butter and sugar, Sukey. Josh, grate the nutmegs and mace, and sift them with the flour. Billy, make ready the hoops. And that leaves you, Sam, to help me separate the eggs. Count 'em out ready: thirty-two for the first baking.'

The three outsize mixing bowls were waiting on the table,

each bigger than the church font. Susannah weighed out butter and precious sugar for each. Josh weighed, spiced and sifted the flour; Billy lined the hoops with strips of paper and made the parchment bases on which they would stand. Then the three of them began to work the butter by hand. When it was soft and creamy, they beat in the sugar, spoons slapping as steadily as a millwheel's paddles. Abram and Sam had begun beating the egg-whites in the copper basins. St Nicholas's chimed the hour, and Susannah saw Abram glance up. They had to repeat the whole process twice through each day, so keeping up to time was vital. Her mother and Harriet were busy clearing out the rooms over the bakeshop, a task Susannah was glad to escape, however tired her wrists and arms might become.

Abram and Sam whisked the egg-whites until the basins could be safely upturned with no risk of the foam's falling out, and then they folded it into the butter and sugar mixture. Josh and Susannah began to beat the yolks. They beat hard for ten minutes; then Abram and Billy took over for ten minutes more. They changed places five times through before the yolks were thick and creamy enough to meet with Abram's approval.

'That should do,' he said at last. 'Ready to set-in, Col?'

'Aye, sir.'

'Good. Sam, fetch the brandy wine.'

They beat in the egg-yolks and the flour, added the brandy, and last of all, handful by handful, tipped in the currants and raisins, the almonds and peel. They were all sweating and tired now. The bakehouse was stifling hot, and the brandy fumes made Susannah's head swim. Col fetched a bucket of water from the well and replenished the bowls of water which stood on the hearths to moisten the air and fend off dizziness. The splashing of the water made her thirsty but she dared not stop. Studded with eight pounds' weight of fruit and almonds, the mixture was now so stiff that she discarded the spoon in favour of the broad wooden paddle, and even so had to use both hands.

Abram said, 'Sam, ask the Missus if she'd like to give it a stir. Them girls too, maybe.'

They crowded into the bakehouse: Mrs Oliver, Harriet and Martha, Pru, Cassy and the girls, old Will. Each and every one of them stirred the mixture and made a wish for Polly.

Abram and Josh spooned it into the hoops in great dollops, rich and spicy, thick with fruit. Col slid the hoops into the ovens and latched the doors shut.

Twenty-seven cakes baking in the ovens; eleven hundred and seventy-three to go.

14

Sugar Under Sail

During that first day they baked fifty-four single-size cakes. Twenty-four days, thought Susannah as she lay in bed that night. Twenty-four days for the baking; then the almond paste; last, the sugar icing to turn them into special-occasion cakes, celebration cakes, proper tributes to the King's Birthday. In the morning she looked into the parlour, to reassure herself by admiring the first batch.

They looked and smelled good: well-risen, shiny brown, spicy and sweet. Fifty-four cakes, drawn up in neat lines on the parlour table – and where could they be stored, dry and cool and safe from mice, while eleven hundred and forty-six more were being baked?

Abram was wondering the same thing. She found him in the pantry, looking at the massive oak crate which hung on chains from the rafters. 'Col had best shift that first batch into the bread crate,' he said, scratching his head. 'It'll take one baking, maybe two, but after that us must think up summat else.'

The work was harder today, lacking yesterday's excitement, and Susannah was glad of the noontime break when the first batch of cakes was safe in the ovens and the second still to be mixed. Her mother and Martha were turning out the linen store which, years ago, had been Aunt Soper's bedroom, so Susannah retreated to the pantry where Polly's friends were singing and chatting as they sieved sugar. Harriet, too, was there, pouring tea for all. 'Parson called,

Miss Sukey,' she said, 'and if the choirboys can be any help, you've only to say. Though I daresay they'd eat as many currants as they cleaned, so it might be a costly offer.' She glanced up as the bread-car chains squeaked. 'I only hope that's not going to come thundering down on our heads. Killed by cakes, that's no epitaph for a good Christian lass. Old Will reckons his shipyard friends might come up with some notion, so he's gone off to the alehouse to see what they can suggest. Well, you never know.'

To Susannah's surprise, Will's enquiries bore fruit. On the following day Christopher Tree sent a couple of workmen who rigged hammocks all over the bakery. Susannah found one of them driving a hook into the lintel of the dole door. Jerking his thumb at the bundle of netting lying along the passage wall, he said, 'To keep your cakes safe 'n snug, missy. Should fool the mice, anyways, but if'n I stood in your shoes I'd give them cats free run a' the place besides. Rats be proper cunning creatures.'

Abram was in the yard with old Will, Mr Tree's Master Carpenter, and Timothy Stenning the cooper. They had an old capstan from the shipyard, a huge wooden hoop, and a bale of miller's gauze, and were deep in plans for rigging up an outsize sieve. 'Get a dozen choirboys to ply it,' Abram explained to Susannah, 'and reckon they'd do more work than twice that number with one tam sieve a-piece. But we'd best pray for fine calm weather.'

'Don't you fret over wind or rain,' the carpenter said. 'Us can cope with that.'

He brought Mr Tree's sailmakers to rig a canvas roof over the yard, to the fascination of the neighbours. Standing in the darkened yard beside Abram, staring up at the taut sailcloth, Susannah said that she half-hoped it *would* rain, to make all the effort worthwhile; and a moment later, taking her by surprise, a small dark shadow skimmed overhead and plopped on the canvas. But it wasn't rain: intrigued by this strange new roof, the cats were padding and sliding and catching their claws in the sail.

The choir trooped cheerfully up Simnel Street and jostled for places at the capstan. It was linked to the great sieve by an array of ropes and blocks; as the boys thrust at the capstan bars, the ropes were pulled tight, the sieve tipped to and fro, and a cloud of sugar sifted through the mesh on to a bed-sheet. It was hot in the yard, under the canvas roof, but the boys seemed to enjoy themselves, stripping off their shirts, kicking off their shoes, and singing sea-shanties at the tops of their voices. 'I daresay it makes a change from hymns and anthems,' Parson remarked, listening with interest. The choir sieved a snowdrift of sugar and feasted on currant buns, and next day there was a crowd of children at the yard gate, all volunteering to try. Will kept a stern eye on them, and though there were several scuffles, and some hasty licks of sugar, they did very well. The girls in the pantry sighed with relief and began work on grinding 140 pounds of almonds. Cassy's grandfather sent a gallon of rose water to counteract the almonds' oiliness, and this made the task of milling easier.

Abram and Susannah and the apprentices worked on. Some of the cakes were lopsided, some were sad, some 'caught' so that Sam had to scrape away the charred surface; but all were honest cakes, made from good fresh ingredients, and all were duly wrapped and stored in the hammocks, now so full that they creaked overhead like rigging in a stiff wind at sea.

On the evening of the day when the thousandth cake came out of the ovens, Attorney Standish called at the house with a lease sticking out of his pocket. 'Now, ma'am, your mind is fixed?' he said to Mrs Oliver.

She nodded.

'And you will vacate the house by the first of June?'

99

She nodded again.

Mr Standish looked up, as if to say she should give a spoken answer, but seeing her face he changed his mind.

'If you'd care to sign, ma'am . . . thank you. And how does the baking progress? It's the talk of the town, I understand. Folk are saying there's not another bakery in the county could rival it.'

Susannah said in surprise, 'You mean it's a matter of – of pride, sir?'

'Certainly. Olivers are townsfolk, born and bred, and this is a mighty enterprise. How much longer, Miss Susannah?'

'Two days more, sir, and then we should begin the almond paste.'

'Ah yes, I've the evidence of my own nose for that. I trust fortune will smile on the work. Indeed, yes.'

The smell of ground almonds pervaded the bakery from the pantry itself, where the girls were doing the grinding, to Susannah's bedroom, three flights higher and the width of the yard away.

'Smells like Furzedown in summer, with a mile a' gorse in full bloom,' Col said longingly next day, sniffing the air. 'Wish us was there.'

'It smells like money,' Susannah said. She could hardly bear to weigh out 140 pounds of sugar for the almond paste. 'Money being ground down to nothing.'

Abram and Sam cracked and separated four hundred and twenty eggs, dropping the yolks into the big mixing bowls and the whites into earthenware crocks which Col carried carefully down to the cellar, the coolest place in the house. Hour after hour, Susannah and Josh and Billy mixed ground almonds, egg-yolks and sugar to a stiff yellow paste. Abram rolled out the paste and trimmed it to fit while Sam brushed the waiting cakes with honey, and then he wrapped it deftly round them and set aside the scraps.

Because the almond paste must dry out before the icing was applied, the cakes could not be dumped back in the hammocks. Every table was filled, every shelf, every cupboard. Col went round the yard, borrowing planks; Will got fifty barrels from Nye's Brewery, and as many casks from his alehouse friends; and together they set up makeshift stands wherever they could find room. By the time the almond paste was finished, two days later, there were cakes everywhere, from Susannah's bedroom to the cellar. Josh told his brother Tom to spread the word, and a hundred boys presented themselves at the dole door, eager to earn sixpence a night by taking it in turns to sit up, candle in hand, through the hours of darkness, on guard against mice. The cats prowled the bakery all night long, fur standing on end, stiff as a chimney-sweep's brushes, but even so, Susannah heard mice squeaking and scrabbling all through her dreams.

On the following day they began beating the egg-whites with Jonathan's silver knives, and weighing out a mountain of sugar, sieved three times through. There were seven hundred egg-whites in all, and Jonathan's words rang in his daughter's head: 'For ten egg-whites, an hour's beating.' When at last the whites had been beaten to a stiff foam, they could begin to beat in the sugar, a spoonful at a time. They worked in shifts of fifteen minutes' beating followed by fifteen minutes' rest, and for the first time Susannah glimpsed what her father meant when he said, 'Reckon good tools and good mates mean as much to the baking as fresh flour and sweet yeast.'

Cassy and the other girls began work on the ornaments for the cakes. They coloured the left-over scraps of almond paste deep red with liquid carmine (Cousin Henniker's gift) and twirled them into rosebuds. Pru Trower came into the bakehouse holding a basket as if not sure what it contained. 'That Chance girl brought this into the shop a few minutes since, bold as a bullfinch, and said, "Susannah might find these useful". So there you are, Sukey my dear, and what's in it the Lord knows.'

The basket was full of leaves, hundreds of green-paper leaves, carefully cut out, and veined with a bodkin. Barbary and the other girls in the millinery workrooms had made them in stolen moments. Armed with these, Polly's friends made up tray after tray of 'roses', each with an almond-paste bud, a paper leaf, and a toasted almond thorn. 'Red roses for King George's Birthday,' Mrs Oliver said, 'nothing could be better.'

The icing was ready at last: thick and white and glossy. Susannah dolloped a spoonful on her first cake and smoothed it with the broad-bladed knife. Abram and Josh and Billy were all quicker than she, each beginning a third cake while she was still anxiously smoothing her first, but she kept up as best she could, and was warmed by their praise.

Col had fired 'King Harry' to dry the air. As each cake was finished, Sam added a red-rose decoration to the damp icing and carried it to the proving table. From time to time Abram tested the icing with his finger. When he judged it right, he nodded to Col. 'Fetch the Missus,' he said.

He gave Mrs Oliver the beechwood marker. She said, 'I'm obliged to you, Abram,' and stamped the clover trademark firmly in the icing. She signed her message to Polly twelve hundred times over.

It took six days to complete the sugar-icing. On the last evening, when only the four great cakes remained, the apprentices set off down the alley, weary from the day's work. Col led the way, surefooted in the dark as any gipsy; Josh steered a sleepy Sam; and Billy brought up the rear, whistling *Spanish Ladies*, soft and slow. Abram, too, had gone home, leaning on Pru's arm, and old Will was at his favourite alehouse on the Hard, standing drinks to the sailmakers. Susannah closed the yard gate and went back into the bakehouse to snuff the candles. It was warm there, warm and dark and quiet. The daybook was waiting on the table, quill and inkwell and penknife beside it. She sat down in the rocker for a moment or two, and fell fast asleep, waking with a start to find her mother looking down on her, candle in hand.

'It's close on midnight, Susan – no, don't get up yet. Harriet's making a pot of tea to revive us.' She sat down, looking weary. 'Mr Gooding has agreed to supply a dozen tea-chests for packing the cakes.'

'Free of charge?' Susannah asked hopefully.

'Tea-dealing is a trade that suits Joseph Gooding,' Mrs Oliver said. 'You can measure out the goods a speck at a time – no risk of having to give a customer a whole bread roll as makeweight. No, Susan, *not* free. But we needn't pay down cash either. He'll take his payment in cakes come Christmas – gifts for his Eastcliff customers.'

'Is that his latest notion?' Susannah asked. Last Christmas Mr Gooding had paid a dozen children to walk the streets all day long, singing a new carol:

> *Now Christ was in a manger born*
> *And God dwelt in a bush of thorn*
> *Which bush of thorn must surely be*
> *The same that yields J. Gooding's tea.*

'So I gather.'

'What sort of cakes?'

'Plum cakes, my dear. With almond paste and sugar icing.'

Harriet came in with the tea-tray. Martha was deep asleep, she said, but she herself felt wakeful as any night-bird. Susannah swallowed a mouthful of tea and let her eyes close. Her mother and Harriet were talking about the move from the house into the bakery. She must have slept again, for she woke in the small hours, refreshed, to find herself still in the rocker, with the quilt off the apprentice's truckle bed over her knees, and her mother asleep in Jonathan's chair. The candle had burned down to a knuckle-end and the flame was guttering. She got up, yawning, to fetch a new candle from the box on the wall.

The daybook still lay on the table. She reached for the quill, meaning to scrawl a few words to record the icing of twelve hundred cakes, but the ink in the well had dried up. She turned the pages, reading the familiar names. *Took as apprentice Samuel Iden son of Widow Iden of Tanner's Yard . . . Nicholas Patching to serve as brushwood boy . . . Accepted William Chennell as apprentice his term as brushwood boy being duly completed . . . Took as apprentice Joshua son of James Herring of Bell Yard . . . .* There were other names, too, remembered from her childhood, and then, further back, names unknown to her except from occasional remarks exchanged between Jonathan and Abram. *Took as apprentice my son Jonathan to serve seven years,* Grandfather Oliver had written, and below his signature had added, *Exceeding proud.* But she had to turn back another twenty years before she came on an entry that said, *Abram Trower from St Stephen's, to serve as baker's man.*

She turned the pages back again, reading the recipes. *Gipsy Bread* – what was that? It had treacle in it, and ginger, and raisins. She must ask Col if the furze-cutters ever baked it. *Rise-up Buns, a thousand, for Ascension Day:* that would appeal to Abram. *Canterbury Huffkins, Arundel Manchets,* and then, catching her eye, *Baked for the great dinner in honour of King George's coronation* – A thousand men, women and children had dined in St Stephen's Fields, and Grandfather had baked three hundred quartern loaves, a thousand revel buns, and – yes – fifty great plum cakes.

She left the book open at that entry, meaning to read it to

Abram, and lay back in the rocker. She drifted off to sleep again, thinking of Grandfather Oliver at his grand baking in this same bakehouse, half a century ago. The watchman tramped down the alley. 'Past three o'clock,' he was calling. 'Past three o'clock, and a fine May night, and all's well.'

Abram arrived early to begin icing the four great cakes. 'Now, Sukey love,' he said, 'reckon us might ask that Chance girl to trim them. Your Mam don't care for her much, I daresay – well, my Pru's the same – but she's got clever fingers, right enough, and as for Hetty Jackson, that calls herself "Madam Henriette", she'd allow her the time off, no question, for the pride of saying one of her girls had trimmed a cake for the King.'

So Susannah fetched out the last of the precious store of red rose petals Jonathan had candied the summer before, and talked her mother into writing a note to Madam Henriette. She delivered it herself, and Madam pursed her mouth for form's sake – 'The workroom's exceeding busy, I fear' – but was ready to be gracious: 'Well, perhaps, as it's for such a patriotic purpose.' She waved Susannah through to the workroom, where Barbary seemed highly amused by the request.

'A cake for Farmer George, you say?' she asked, using the King's nickname in a way that would have scandalized her employer.

'And one for the Prince Regent, and one for the Duke of York, and one for Lord Wellington out in the Peninsula. Will you help?'

'Well now. There are six bonnets promised for next week, you know. *Faithfully* promised. Farmer George's sons ought to wait their turn – and it might do them good at that,' Barbary said. 'But Wellington's another matter. A rifleman told me they'd sooner see his long nose in a fight than have a thousand reinforcements at their back. Any little service that's to his benefit . . . And at your Mam's request – that's the gilt on the gingerbread, I must admit. I'll bring my workbox.'

All day long Barbary shut herself in the office, occasionally opening the door to call for more almond paste – more carmine colouring – gilt paper – thin red ribbon – copper wire. While she worked, the apprentices were wrapping the single-size cakes in paper and sealing each with a blob of wax, on which Susannah stamped the bakery mark. They were packed into Mr Gooding's tea-chests, snugly padded with flour sacks; a Revenue officer came to check and approve them; and as he watched, old Will nailed down the lids. Abram and Will corded each chest, and Susannah sealed the knots. The cargo was packed and ready.

Barbary worked on. Martha tried to peep through the keyhole, but Barbary had stopped it up with almond paste. Not until dusk did she open the door to let them see the masterpieces.

She had decked the Royal cakes, very properly, with red roses, adding gilt-paper crowns for King George, plumes for the Prince Regent, lions for the Duke of York. Martha gasped in awe. But Wellington's cake was different. When Pru Trower saw it, her face broke into a smile. Then she hesitated. 'It's exceedingly clever, but – well –'

Barbary had decorated the cake with crossed swords cut out of silver paper and crowned it with a vivid garland of flowers fashioned from paper and almond paste. Not roses, though: these were wild flowers, their green leaves deftly snicked and curled, their petals ranging from coral pink to crimson.

Mrs Oliver said, 'Red clover, I see. The bakery trademark.'

'Bee Bread,' Pru said. 'That's what old Mr Oliver allus called it.'

'And red campion – Soldier Boys,' Barbary said, watching

their expressions as she used the country nickname. 'And ragged robin, of course – Polly Baker.'

And scarlet pimpernel too, Susannah noticed. Shepherd's Joy and Polly Baker. She saw the glint in Barbary's eyes.

'Although the cake's your gift to Lord Wellington and his staff officers,' Barbary said, 'I daresay there'll be a soldier to get the crate open and a batman to hand the slices round – *and* lift a piece for himself, and tell his fellows how it looked and how it tasted. Laurels and bays and such-like classical fancies would leave him cold, but Soldier Boys and Bee Bread and the rest, they'll speak loud and clear. The tale will be round the ranks in the blink of an eye.'

'Quite so,' Mrs Oliver said. 'I'm obliged to you.'

She inclined her head. Barbary winked at Susannah.

'Well, it's a fine bit of work, no one could deny that,' Pru said, as if she wished she could, 'but will it last the journey?'

Barbary shrugged. 'That's in other hands.'

'Easy said, but – Well, no matter,' Pru said. 'No sense saying more, when there it is, and as bonny a garland as ever – We'll do the best we can.'

15

The Harbour Side Is Crowded

The following morning, the household yawned over its work. Abram and Will went down to the Hard to see the tea-chests safely stowed aboard *Constant Anne*. Mrs Oliver had said to Pru, 'Put the three Royal cakes in the shop window for today, the town deserves a glimpse,' but when Susannah stepped into the street she was disappointed to find no one there admiring them, not even the children. She went indoors again, and tried to add up the accounts in the office, but found this so depressing that she retreated to the bakehouse where the apprentices were clearing up after the morning's work, listless and in low spirits.

Her mother appeared shortly before noon, tying the ribbons of her London bonnet. 'Pru is closing the shop and coming down to see the ship weigh anchor,' she said, 'and Harriet and Martha are putting on their cloaks. Joshua, if you three want to come – yes, and the boy too – you're very welcome. Susan, could you fetch a cheese from the store-room? I did think of giving Mr Beamish one of your father's keeper cakes, but it wouldn't be the best of gifts for a man with sugar sickness.'

The Market Place was empty, Fore Street virtually deserted; all the shops had their shutters up or their blinds drawn. 'Surely they can't all be on the quayside,' Mrs Oliver said. 'It isn't possible –' But when she emerged from the Sea Gate, she saw that there indeed they were, every man and woman and child in town, lining the harbour side, crowding the Sea Steps. People squeezed aside good-naturedly to let the bakery party through, and bit by bit they worked their way down towards the Hard. Susannah glanced around her, catching sight of Cousin Henniker and Cassy and her grandfather – Christopher Tree – Solomon Nye from the brewery – Miller Challen – Josh's mother and all his sisters – Mr Chartman, the *Courant*'s editor – Attorney Standish – a cluster of Polly's friends – the old waiter from Myngs –

As Mrs Oliver stepped on to the Hard, she said, 'I don't know when I last saw such a crowd.'

'Not since word came of the great victory at Trafalgar,' Parson said, overhearing her, 'and they brought Lord Nelson's body home. Mr Mayor's going to have trouble getting through.'

Susannah glanced back, up the crowded Steps, to glimpse the Mayor's scarlet robes. 'And Banker Pratt, too, just behind him,' she said.

'And the first shall be last,' Parson said. 'Very apt. Joseph Gooding, now, *there's* a man who looks ahead. He sent two hand-picked shopmen down an hour since with orders to secure pride of place. But come along, Susannah – your mother will want a word with the lieutenant.'

The crowd parted to let them make their way along the Hard to *Constant Anne*'s mooring. Two seamen, armed with muskets, were posted on the Hard, and another at the head of the gangway. 'Very sensible,' said the harbour-master, who was watching the preparations. 'Morning, ma'am. Morning, Parson sir. *Constant Anne*, ahoy! Tell the captain the owner's here.'

Mr Beamish came ashore. He was a haggard young man, painfully thin, with a sickly complexion and a stern, grim manner. There was a difficult voyage ahead of him: a crew unfit for active service, a ship hastily fitted out, a cargo to make any naval man split his sides laughing. He touched his hat to Mrs Oliver and kept his mouth tight shut.

'The letters of authority and the permits,' she said, handing them over.

'Ma'am.'

'And a cheese for the voyage.'

'I'm obliged to you, ma'am.'

'The cakes are safely aboard?'

'They are.'

'Nothing remains but to wish you Godspeed.'

'Ma'am.'

'Never saw a man who put me so much in mind of a herring,' the harbour-master remarked as Mr Beamish returned on board. 'Nothing to him but ribs and backbone and a cold eye. Daresay he didn't reckon with such a crowd to cheer him on his way, but folk want to make an occasion of it, right enough. Parson tells me he has it in mind to read a verse or two from Scripture, and I'd lay a pound to a penny Mr Mayor's got a speech tucked in his sleeve.'

Susannah looked round, scanning the crowd. The Mayor was still trying to force his way down the Steps. 'Tide won't wait,' the harbour-master said cheerfully. 'Best make a start, Parson sir.'

Parson took a Bible out of his pocket and said mildly, to those around him, 'Well now, friends, we'll have a short reading from Holy Writ and a psalm to ask a blessing on the voyage.'

The onlookers crowding the harbour wall, standing their ground on the Steps, leaning over the ramparts far above, could not hear him, but those in earshot did, and as they cleared their throats and shuffled their feet, the women hushing their children, the men pulling off their hats, so the quiet spread slowly outwards and upwards. Mr Beamish's voice rang out curtly: 'Carry on, Mr Mate,' he said, disregarding the ceremonies on the harbour side. Parson's reading was punctuated by shouted orders, running feet on the deck, the thrum of rope and chain: but he went on, unperturbed, with the Lammas verses:

'And the Lord spake unto Moses saying, Speak unto the children of Israel and say unto them, When ye come into the land whither I bring you, then it shall be that, when ye eat of the bread of the land, ye shall offer up an offering unto the Lord. Ye shall offer up a cake of the first of your dough for an offering. Of the first of your dough ye shall give unto the Lord an offering in your generations.'

The choirboys sang the Seamen's Psalm as *Constant Anne* slipped her moorings and ghosted across the Inner Harbour. The crowd craned to watch her, and as the psalm ended they burst into shouts of 'Huzza!' and flung their hats in the air. The ship's sails filled and stiffened. Ahead of her lay the grey Channel, the Bay of Biscay, the Atlantic coast of the Peninsula and, God willing, the quays of Lisbon. She lifted on the swell of the open sea.

The crowd broke up. People went back to work, chivvying their children ahead of them. Mrs Oliver was talking with Mrs Verney and Mrs Tree. 'Why cake, though, Dorothy?' one asked her gently.

'Polly went without our consent,' Mrs Oliver said, 'I didn't want her to go without our blessing.'

Susannah followed them towards the Sea Steps, and careful though Parson's choice of Scripture had been, it seemed to her that the song the boatmen were singing along the quays made a truer farewell:

> *As I walked out one morning*
> *In the springtime of the year,*
> *I overheard a sailor boy,*
> *Likewise a lady fair.*
>
> *Said the sailor to the lady*
> *'We soon must sail away,*
> *And it's lovely on the water*
> *To hear the music play.'*

His sweetheart fell and fainted
And soon they brought her to,
They both shook hands together
And took their fond adieu.

The harbour side is crowded
With mothers weeping sore
For their sons are gone to face the foe
Whereas the cannon roar.

16

From the Far Far Coast of Portugal

The three great cakes were dispatched to London, where
Susannah's Aunt Soper took charge of them with a proper
sense of their importance. The bakery settled into a quieter
routine: bread, rolls and buns daily; Madeira cakes and
macaroons on card-party nights; gingerbread on Saturdays.
After the strain and weariness of the great cake-baking,
Susannah found she could cope quite well with the
everyday tasks of writing up the daybook, keeping the
accounts, and taking turns with Sam as assistant to Josh and
Billy. The takings were steady – 'Enough to cover the wages
and the bills,' she said when Abram asked her, 'but no profit
to set against the cost of the cakes. Still, the rent should
help.'

The Bagots moved in on the first of June. Mrs Oliver and
Harriet had spring-cleaned the house from top to bottom,
turned the office into a parlour and the store-room into a
dining-closet, and emptied the attic over the shop for
Susannah. When she woke up on the second of June, it took
her a moment to remember where she was. She dressed and
went downstairs to the new dining-closet, which was just
large enough for a table and chairs, with Mrs Oliver's china
ranged on the shelves where Jonathan had stored his
conserves, and a little window knocked in the south wall to
admit a haze of June sunlight. The Bagots were hiring the
maids as well as the house, on the understanding that

Harriet would cook for both households, and Martha today was in a sad flutter at the thought of waiting on Miss Bagot – 'She looks proper particular, Miss Sukey,' she said dolefully, 'all starched and sewn up, never a pin about her.'

Mrs Oliver said, 'After breakfast, Susan, we should call, and ask if everything's as they wish. Front door, of course.'

It was strange to go through the shop and down Simnel Street to the little cobbled court; strange to mount the half-moon steps and knock at their own front door; strange to be admitted by Martha, twisting her hands in her apron, and shown into the trim and shining parlour where Miss Bagot awaited them. Mrs Oliver looked as if she had taken a dose of medicine, as yet unswallowed; Miss Bagot peered at Susannah and said, 'Of course, my poor dear brother does *not* care for children, after thirty years at the thankless task of teaching idle boys'; Mr Bagot himself did not appear.

Two days later, on the fourth of June, Billy baked gingerbread kings for the Birthday Fair. As she dried the baking sheets and stacked them on their shelf, Susannah was wondering about the cakes. Had they reached Lisbon? Or were they being nibbled by fishes at the bottom of the sea? Billy wiped the gingerbread mould with a clean dry cloth and said to her, 'Want to have a try at the gilding?'

'Are you sure, Billy?'

'Bolt the pantry door,' Billy said, 'shut the window – and don't go breathing! A light touch and a steady hand, that's all it takes.'

Susannah found she enjoyed brushing egg-white on each crown and sword, and touching them with gold leaf, light as gossamer. The gilt shone bravely against the glossy dark gingerbread. Down by the river in St Stephen's Fields the children were building booths of green branches. Girls and their sweethearts would walk there in the evening sunlight and buy fairings for one another – bright cotton handkerchiefs from Osborne's 'house', sugar pigs from Bullus's, gingerbreads from Oliver's.

'I told our Tom to pick out the best site, by the ford,' Josh said, as he and Susannah packed the gilded kings into baskets. 'And with young Col to help him build the house, there's a chance it'll stand up this year – not like last,' he added, grinning. 'You know Kitty Bristow – Banker Pratt's housemaid?'

'Yes, of course. Her banns were read out in church on Sunday.'

'She called at the shop this morning and asked Miss Pru if'n Oliver's would bake the bride-cake and the wedding favours. And Banker's told her to order three dozen queen cakes and three dozen tartlets as well, at his expense. Can you order another sugar loaf, Miss Sukey? And more gold leaf – Billy says we're running low.'

'Who supplies it?' Susannah asked, reaching for the slate.

'Jacob Spalding – the carver and gilder. Has a cottage down by the shipyards. He trims the nobs' cabins and brightens up the figureheads.'

Susannah turned up the queen-cake recipe in the daybook, to check the other ingredients. 'Sugar and flour,' she read, 'butter, eggs, currants, nutmeg, mace and cinnamon –'

'Queen cakes,' said a voice from the doorway, 'and I could down half a dozen fresh-baked, here and now.' And there stood Jonathan, one hand gripping the doorpost for support.

'Da, oh Da –'

'There now, there now, Sukey love. Take it gently.'

He lowered himself into the rocking-chair, coughing painfully. His jawbone jutted through his skin, and his cheeks were hollow, there were sores on his hands and throat, and he looked as flaccid as a plant straggling in a cellar. But he was alive, he was home. Susannah ran for her mother. 'Come quick, Mam – Da's here, in the bakehouse – no news of Polly, or at least he's said nothing – but he's here, truly here, he's home.'

Jonathan had sent two long letters from Portugal, but both must have gone astray. After several weeks of enquiring and searching in Lisbon, he had got permission to join a party of volunteers, newly arrived from England, going up to the lines. It proved to be a bleak journey. Cold, hungry, eaten alive by fleas, they had struggled through the mountains in pursuit of the Army. They came on a village which had been burned by the enemy a few days before, and three days' march further on, another; but they trudged on until the fever struck them. Within twenty-four hours most of the men were down with it, Jonathan among them. The few able-bodied men dragged them to a group of shepherds' huts overlooking the track and did their best to care for them there.

'I lost all sense of time,' Jonathan said, 'but we were still alive, by God's mercy, when a train of waggons came down the track, carrying sick and wounded down to Lisbon. They lifted us in among the rest, and when that waggon started down the track I wished they'd left me to die – now, Dorothy love, don't upset yourself. How the wounded survived the journey, only God could tell. The soldiers were good to us, main good – gave us water, wrapped us up as best they could, and when we reached Lisbon, took me to the Army hospital with the rest and did all they could for me.'

When the fever ebbed, days later, he had no strength left. He had crawled through the dormitories asking every man there if he knew Dick Fletching, but with no success. But many of the sick and wounded soldiers had asked him to take messages for their own families at home – 'I scribbled them down in my pocket book,' he said, 'if I read out the names, Sukey love, and tell you what to put, we could at least send their kin a word –'

'Tomorrow,' Mrs Oliver said firmly, 'not a moment sooner, and then only if Dr Craik approves. Rest, my dear, get back your strength, and then we had best tell you all that's been happening here at home while you were beyond seas.'

17

A Lesson Learned

It took Jonathan several weeks to recover ('As much from
your Mam's plan as from the Spanish fever,' he said) but the
morning after his return he made his way to the bakehouse,
and from then on he was there every day at dawn, kneading
the dough and shaping the loaves, instructing the
apprentices, talking to Abram, and generally winning back
his strength.

To Susannah's dismay, though, no sooner was Jonathan
feeling more himself than he realized she should be at
school. 'You've missed months, love – I know it couldn't be
helped, and I'm grateful as can be, but it's a crying shame
you should have had to do it. Now, I'll have a word with
Miss Honeywood this very day, and away you go come
Monday.'

'But, Da –'

'No, no, my dear. We can manage here. You get back to
your lessons.'

So Susannah went back to Miss Honeywood's parlour
where her sampler waited, untouched for half a year. The
other girls greeted her amiably, and she settled back into the
routine of plain sewing, embroidery, copying lace patterns,
learning verses by heart, singing scales. But her thoughts
kept straying to the bakehouse where every hour of work
showed an end result and every penny spent had its
purpose.

One morning Miss Honeywood took her pupils to collect

shells on the Eastcliff beach. As they were walking home past the Eastcliff villas, Susannah hung back, thinking she might see Harriet's sister. But it was Barbary Chance who strolled into view, swinging a hatbox in her hand. Susannah was truly pleased to see her.

'What, allowed out – under escort, at least?' Barbary said. 'And how are you, Susannah?'

'Feeling hedged in,' Susannah said ruefully, and Barbary laughed, remembering. It was a clear ringing laugh and several heads turned, but luckily Miss Honeywood was conversing with the older girls and did not look back.

'Though the words stick in my throat,' Barbary remarked, 'I may have been a trifle hard on your Mam. A touch too severe, you know – just a touch. You can scramble over a hedge if need be. Push your way through it. Uproot it by main force. But you see those chits peeping down at us?' She gestured to the top-storey windows of the villa they were passing. 'Fine dresses, silk stockings, the most stylish bonnets you could find south of London Town, and certain sure they'll never starve'–*but* they daren't go in the open air for fear the sun will brown their complexions, daren't raise their voices, daren't speak to anyone without a proper introduction. Not that they'd know what to do with freedom if they had it. Ah well, your own gaoler's peering at me round the brim of that remarkable bonnet. Tell her I was asking you where in the world she got those purple felt pansies – I'm all agog to know.'

She went swiftly up the hill, whistling like an errand boy, and Susannah smiled as she watched her go. All that afternoon, as they sorted their shells and arranged them in prim patterns to frame the seaside sketches they had drawn the week before, Susannah sat quiet. Miss Honeywood had reproved her for chattering with Barbary – 'An unfortunate girl, I admit, but with no more idea of proper manners than the kitchen cat' – and was pleased to see her silent, thinking she was taking her words to heart. So she was, but not in the way Miss Honeywood had intended. When she got home, she sought out Jonathan, who was in the pastry room, making almond-paste decorations for the Mayor's St Swithin's supper.

'Da,' she said, 'I'm wasting my time at school – my time and your money. I've outgrown Miss Honeywood's parlour in these past few months. I can't sit quiet there for three years more.'

'I promised your Mam you girls should have proper schooling.'

'I can read and write, Da love, and sew and keep household accounts. Where's the sense in paying down good money to go on practising those things in that stuffy parlour, month after month, when I could be putting them to real use here at home?'

'I could speak to your Mam,' Jonathan said at last, 'but I know she'll be against it.'

'But if she did agree –'

'Then I suppose I would agree likewise.'

When Jonathan told his wife that Susannah wanted to give up her lessons, she at first said nothing.

'Well, Dorothy my dear, what do you think?'

'I suppose we must let her have her way.'

So Susannah left Miss Honeywood's and stayed at home. She helped Mrs Oliver with the household work, for Harriet and Martha had their hands full with the Bagots, who paid their rent promptly, and kept themselves to themselves, but were extremely particular. Everything must be kept just so, and never a sound made above a whisper. Miss Bagot bought Martha a pair of felt slippers in which to shuffle around the house; Mr Bagot stopped the chiming clock, and oiled all the doors every Monday; and when the children came from house to house singing for pennies on their Midsummer rounds, Martha was sent out with a shilling piece on condition that they went away at once.

When Lieutenant Beamish rapped at the front door to report *Constant Anne's* safe return, Martha flapped through the hall in the felt slippers and let out such a squeal of excitement on seeing him that Harriet came running from the kitchen. 'Mrs Oliver, sir?' Martha was saying. 'Oh but they're not living here just at present because of hiring out the house, you see – oh if you please, sir, is there any news? Though I suppose you wouldn't tell me, not before them, and quite right too, but –'

Harriet said, 'Show the gentleman to the shop, Martha, and quick about it, while I tell Miss Bagot there's no riot at the door, and the house hasn't caught fire, and she needn't be fretting.'

Mr Beamish gave Mrs Oliver a receipt signed by the Commissariat in Lisbon and told her that the cakes had been dispatched in a train of supply waggons going up the lines. 'Thieves, brigands and Frenchmen willing, they should reach the regiment, ma'am.'

Jonathan asked Christopher Tree to sell *Constant Anne*. For two weeks more the ship lay alongside the Hard while Mr Tree made enquiries for a buyer. Susannah walked down to look at her, and remembered how full the days had been during the grand cake-baking.

18

The Dole Door

Lammas came and went; Michaelmas; Harvest Home. The numbers of people waiting at the dole door each morning increased as the autumn drew on, and sometimes vagabonds slept there overnight, huddled against the warm bricks of the bakehouse wall. Susannah came to dread the moment of unbolting the door in the morning, and handed out the bread as quickly as she could. On the morning of the first hard frost, a bitter November day, she gave the dole early, while the bread was still warm. At the end of the line was a woman wearing a big frieze cloak and hood. Susannah reached into the basket for a loaf, not looking up; then a voice said, 'No – please –', and she glanced up, astonished, not daring to believe what her ears told her, and saw that it was Polly.

For a moment neither of them moved. Then they were hugging each other, arms wrapped tightly round one another's waists, cheek against cheek so that Susannah smelled the cold on Polly's skin. 'Quick,' she said, 'come inside, you must be near frozen –'

Jonathan was in the bakehouse, mixing macaroons. He looked up to see them. Polly put back her hood. 'Sukey,' he said, his voice thickening, 'fetch your Mam quick. Oh Polly love –'

Susannah ran up to the bedroom, found it empty, ran down again to the little dining-parlour. 'It's Polly, Mam – Polly's come home. She's in the bakehouse with Da.'

Mrs Oliver set down the coffee pot, tucked a lock of hair under her cap, took off and folded her apron and laid it over her chair. She went along the passage to the bakehouse. Polly was lying back in the old rocking-chair, looking drawn and tired. She and her mother looked at one another, and Mrs Oliver bent over her to kiss her forehead.

'Well, Polly,' she said, 'you're tired out, and no wonder. But your hair – Why in the world have you had it cropped? You look like something from the poorhouse. Lice, was it, aboard ship? May that be a lesson to you. Stand up, do, let me take a proper look. Yes, well, it's no wonder you're worn out, racketing across the ocean with a baby coming – and well on its way, by the look of you. When is it due?'

'In a month's time, Mam,' Polly said.

'Then you should take better care of yourself. Sit down, sit down, take the weight off your feet. Warm some milk over the fire, Jonathan, and find some fresh bread rolls. Where's the boy? Ah, good,' she said as Sam came whistling in from the yard, 'no need to stare, Samuel, your eyes tell you true – slip on your jacket and run to tell Mr Trower, and then ask Dr Craik to call. Then to Mr Woodling's to tell Mrs Dorcas – yes, and see Mr Henniker has the news too.'

'I'll tell Pru,' Susannah said, and slipped out of the bakehouse. She waylaid Sam at the gate and told him to call at Madam Henriette's and leave a message for Barbary – 'Just say all's well, nothing more' – and herself ran to the shop to tell Pru, who sat down with a thump on the stool. 'The Lord be praised, Sukey love. Does my Da know?'

'Sam ran to tell him first of all.'

Susannah went back to the bakehouse where Jonathan was saying, 'Now, Polly my dear, we've a deal to ask you – yes, and to tell. But first and foremost, you found Dick Fletching?'

'Yes, Da, indeed I did. It was a fearful journey,' Polly said, 'but worth it when I reached the lines. I'm sorry, Mam, I know that's hard hearing for you –'

'Never mind,' Mrs Oliver said. 'Go on.'

'Well, at first I had to keep to the rear with the other women, all of us trudging after the Army as best we could. But the wife of one of the officers had come out to join him, and was travelling with the baggage train. She needed a maid, and she offered me the place. I was well-spoken, you see, and could do fine sewing.' She smiled a little. 'Miss Honeywood's teaching stood me in good stead in the end. They were kind to me, Mrs Delahunt and the Major – even agreed to act as the witnesses at our wedding.' She glanced at her mother, and away again. 'It wasn't the wedding you'd have chosen for me, Mam. No church, no brides-maid, no new muslin. But there was a man in the company who'd been a good friend to Dick – Ezra Arkwright, a northerner, a Methodist preacher. We made our vows in front of him, with the Major and his lady as witnesses, and all Dick's mates looking on, and one of the lads made me a ring.' She looked down at the steel ring on her wedding-finger. 'It came off a bit of broken harness, I think. But it served very well. Ezra preached a sermon for us, and wrote my wedding lines in my Bible, and the Delahunts signed them. A drumhead wedding, they called it.'

'And after that?' Jonathan asked her as she sat twisting the steel ring.

'Well, I could see Dick occasionally – when the Army made camp. And being Mrs Delahunt's maid saved me a deal of trouble – the Provost Marshal was forever trying to get us women out from under the Army's feet, he swore we slowed down the march worse than the mud or the wounded. But once Dick knew about the baby, he couldn't rest. Fretting over it ate him raw inside. He hadn't been paid for months, and my money was swallowed up buying food, and a blanket, and ointment for the boils – We were at our wits' end when the cakes came.' She smiled at Jonathan. 'I can't tell you,' she said, 'I can't *tell* you how the rumours flew! Some of the men said it was an enemy ruse – catch the Government sending cake for the likes of us, or the Army handing it over! No, it must be a French plot, and the cakes were laced with wormwood or powdered glass. But when I saw the trademark, I knew better.'

She picked up the beechwood marker from the table, and ran a finger round the carved clover head.

'What happened then, love?' Jonathan asked her.

'I couldn't stop crying – that's what. I sat there staring at the mark stamped in the icing, and sobbing my heart out. And then we heard there were hundreds of those cakes, over a thousand of them, one for every officer and every man in the regiment, and one for Lord Wellington himself with a garland of red clover round it – Da's best bride-cakes from first to last.'

'Did they taste as they ought?' Susannah asked, anxious to know.

'That I can't tell you,' Polly said. 'We sold ours to an officer in the Connaught Rangers – he paid a good price, gladly. A loaf of your fresh bread, Da, would sell for six shillings in camp, to an officer with money of his own to pay for his comforts. Dick's mates, almost all the company, sold theirs too, to the officers of other regiments, and each and every one of them gave us half the money, and that paid the cost of sending me down to Lisbon, and getting me a decent lodging there, and paying my passage home in the *Sophy Croft*. Dick sends his respects, Da,' she said, looking at Jonathan, 'and thanks you with all his heart.'

'That's a good lad,' Jonathan said, 'but it's not me you should be thanking. I went out to Lisbon myself to try for word of you, and failed dismally. Abram baked those cakes, twelve hundred of them, with your sister and the lads to help him, and half the town besides. But it was your Mam who raised the funds, and hired out the house to do it, it was your Mam who travelled up to London and made a proper nuisance of herself to get the needful permits, and the notion from first to last was hers.'

19

Cradle Cake

For several days after Polly's return the bakeshop's trade doubled, with customers queuing up to ask Pru how she was, what had happened, was it true there was a baby coming? 'A daughter of mine, the talk of the town,' Mrs Oliver said disapprovingly, hearing the babble and chatter from the shop. But she welcomed Polly's friends to the little parlour, and dispatched Jonathan to ensure that Christopher Tree and the other men heard a true account. Cousin Henniker came to call, rather shocked, and reluctant to ask questions for fear of what Polly might answer; but he did ask after Dick Fletching, and Polly smiled and thanked him affectionately, and seemed for a moment more like her old self than she had been since her return.

The knowledge that her mother had hired out the house to raise money for the cakes oppressed Polly's spirits, and when Cassy said shyly that she and her grandfather would gladly offer Polly a bed for a few weeks, the bakery being short of space, it was a relief to them all. So Polly moved to Green Street, but walked home to the bakery every day to wash and iron and mend the bakehouse linen, and to sew baby clothes in the parlour. 'Cassy's a good girl,' Mrs Oliver said, 'but mind, I want you home again in good time, before the baby comes.'

So Polly came home on St Catherine's Day when the bakery smelled of mincemeat and spice and hot crisp pastry. A bed was made up in the parlour, to save her the stairs. Two days later, just as the church clock chimed three, Martha came clattering along the passage to the bakehouse, calling for Jonathan. 'Sir, sir, Missus says to send for the midwife, the baby's coming, you're to send straightway if you please, and will Miss Susan go sit with her sister a moment or two and see to it she doesn't fret herself.'

Polly showed no signs of fretting. She was sitting peaceably in the parlour with a packet of letters in her lap.

'I've written a note to Dick, Sukey,' she said. 'Once the baby's born, will you add a line or two, telling him all's well, and see it's sent off? It may not reach him, I know, but at least I shall have tried. And this is Dick's Will, I wrote it out for him before we parted, and he made his mark with Ezra to witness it. And there's a note here for Da and you and Mam, just in case.'

Mrs Oliver came briskly in. 'Now, Susan, there's a long night ahead, I don't doubt, and the best thing you can do to help is to keep your father out of the way. Send the midwife in as soon as she arrives, tell the boy to hold himself ready to go for the doctor, bid Martha bank up the kitchen fire and keep the big kettle simmering, and if anyone comes questioning and prattling, pack them off as best you can.'

Susannah spent the evening in the bakehouse with her father. He mixed the starter dough himself, guiltily – 'Your Mam would never forgive me if she found me up to the elbows in dough on such a night' – and then settled himself in his chair to wait. Billy dozed on the truckle bed, Susannah in the rocker, remembering that other night when she had sat here with her mother.

Shortly before dawn, when Billy was yawning at the kneeler and Jonathan was keeping his hands thrust in his pockets, Harriet looked into the bakehouse and said it was time to call the doctor. Billy ran off down the dark street and twenty minutes later Dr Craik arrived in stately fashion, with his man carrying his bag and a porter to light their way. Martha came pattering across the yard, still in her nightcap, eager for news. Abram arrived a few minutes before Josh and Sam and Col.

'No word yet,' Jonathan told them. 'Doctor's here.'

Abram and the boys got on with the work of kneading and shaping the loaves, and Jonathan watched them, restive and unable to settle.

'You're not planning to bake, then?' Abram said to him.

'And what would my wife say if she found me at it?'

Abram said, 'If'n all goes well, there'll be cradle cake needed.'

Jonathan stared. 'Upon my word – I hadn't thought – it never crossed my mind –'

The birth of a baby meant a string of visits from family and neighbours and friends, who must be greeted with plum cake, ale and sherry wine.

Pulling himself together, Jonathan said, 'Sukey love, the biggest cake hoop. Now, Col lad, in an hour's time I'll need "Daniel" at plum-cake heat –' Comforted by the need to bake, he weighed out butter and sugar, found his favourite spoon and knife, began to cream the mixture. Susannah, too, found it a help to have something to do. She cleaned currants, chopped peel, shredded almonds, and all the while her mind filled with thoughts of Polly, and of Dick far off in Spain.

The bakehouse smelled of fresh-baked bread. The delivery boys came trooping in to eat their breakfasts and collect their baskets. There was a sharp frost, they said; it was a proper winter morning, dark and cold. Tom reached for the pipe. 'What's to play, sir?'

Jonathan thought for a moment. '*High Germany*,' he said. 'That should do.' He hummed as he whisked the eggs:

O Polly, my dear Polly, the rout has now begun
And we must march away by the beating of the drum . . .
And when your pretty babe is born, sits smiling on your knee,
Then think upon your own true love in High Germany.

When the cradle cake was safely in the oven, he began to mix and beat rum butter. Harriet snatched a moment to look into the bakehouse. 'She's taking her time,' she said, 'but all's well. Martha, have you served Mr Bagot's breakfast? And sent up Miss's pot of tea and proper thin bread and butter? Good. Then you'd best get back to the kitchen and fry some bacon nice and crisp, and brew a pot of coffee. Doctor wants a bit of sustenance.'

Nine o'clock struck; ten o'clock; eleven. Jonathan took the cradle cake out of the oven and turned it carefully out of its hoop.

'Jonathan?' It was Mrs Oliver's voice. Susannah jumped up. 'Jonathan? Where *is* the man? Well, my dear, you've a granddaughter, and she's a fine strong child. Polly needs a good sleep, but she'll soon be herself again, thanks be. Now come give Dr Craik a glass of wine, he's mighty pleased with himself but I'm bound to say he's earned his money. Susan, see all the house knows, and then step round to Green Street, there's a good girl.'

Susannah called at the apothecary's and at Cousin Henniker's, and then ran down the alley to Bugle Street. One of the Eastcliff ladies was just being ushered into Madam Henriette's, with three daughters and a governess following in her train; Susannah did not like to interrupt or slip past them into the workroom, but one of the apprentices was holding the shop door and bobbing curtseys to the customers, so she gave her a swift message for Barbary – 'Just say all's well, if you please' – before taking herself home again, tired but content. She could hear a baby wailing fretfully as she crossed the yard – not just any baby, Polly's daughter, her own niece. In the house the bedroom window opened and Miss Bagot looked out suspiciously; this noise, small as it was, could not be paid off with sixpences.

Polly was lying in bed, propped up on pillows, with the

baby snuffling in the crook of her arm. On one side of the bed was the cradle in which she herself had slept as a baby; on the other a table spread with the best cloth, and on it the cradle cake, a bowl of rum butter, a jug of ale. Mrs Oliver was sitting in the chair with a tea-tray beside her.

Polly smiled at her sister. 'Come and meet your niece, Sukey.'

Susannah took the baby carefully into her arms. She was small and crumpled and red, with a fuzz of dark hair. Jonathan came in, kissed Polly, and tickled his grand-daughter's cheek. 'There now, my pretty one – ' He dipped his finger in the rum butter and eased it into her mouth, so that her first taste of food should be sweet and good.

Abram and Pru came in, with a bright new shilling fetched specially from Pratt's Bank, to tuck in the baby's hand, and after them the rest of the household. Harriet was tired but smiling, Martha beaming broadly. Sam hung back, bashful, but Josh bent over the cradle to admire the baby and said to Billy, 'Tips the scales at a good seven pounds, I'd say.' Polly laughed: 'Half a sugar loaf at least,' she said. Will had brought the baby a new horseshoe for luck, and Col one of his elf-bolts from the Downs. They all ate and drank, to wish her health and happiness, and then Mrs Oliver turned them out: 'We'll have half the town here tomorrow, agape for cakes and ale, Polly should sleep while she can.'

Susannah went to the bakehouse and took Polly's letter to Dick out of her pocket. *Brother Dick,* she wrote, *Polly has a daughter, plump and healthy, with dark hair like her own –*

'Are you writing to your Aunt Soper,' Jonathan asked, coming in to find her at the table with quill and inkwell, 'or to your Mam's brothers?'

'To Dick, from Polly.'

'Well, mind you tell him his daughter's a fine healthy child. And write up the daybook too, there's a good girl.'

Susannah said, 'Wouldn't you rather do it, Da?'

'Ah well, you kept the record all the months I was away,' Jonathan said. 'I reckon it's your right.'

Susannah coloured with pleasure. She pulled the daybook towards her and wrote, *Polly's daughter born this morning a little before eleven of the clock. Her father Dick Fletching being with the Army beyond seas. A baking of cradle cake. Great joy.*

Jonathan read it over her shoulder, and nodded. 'Your sister says Dick Fletching's a shepherd born,' he said. 'If he comes home safe from the wars, which God grant, he'll be seeking a place as a shepherd – not setting up shop here. Now, maybe you'll do like your sister, and choose a husband outside the bakery trade. But meanwhile, there's the shop and the bakehouse. I could teach you the way of it.'

Susannah swallowed. 'An apprenticeship, Da?' she said.

'If you wished. Or you could work alongside us, as you go, without a formal agreement.'

'I'd never make a pastrycook, Da. I couldn't bake for the sheer love of it – not as you do.'

'True enough,' Jonathan said. 'Nor did your grandpa. But he ran this bakery as well as it's ever been run.'

Susannah said, 'I did enjoy being part of it. When we were baking the cakes, even though I got tired, I did like to feel I was sharing it all. Yes, and before that, too.'

'We could build on that,' Jonathan said equably. 'Think it over.'

Susannah folded and sealed the letter, and took it down to Myngs. The elderly waiter said several officers bound for Spain were staying in the hotel, he daresaid one of them would carry the letter to Lisbon, and how was the baby?

When she left the hotel, she walked along the ramparts towards the Sea Gate. She went slowly, looking out across the Harbour, and all the while her father's words ran in her head, persistent as the sea.

20

Sung in the Streets

She told Polly about it next day when she was in the parlour, making ready for a stream of callers. Polly said, 'It depends on you, Sukey. It would certainly please Da very much.'

'What about Mam, though?'

'Ah well,' Polly said, 'a year ago Da would never even have suggested it. The thought wouldn't even have crossed his mind. She's surprised him too, I think. There she is, speaking up sharp about what people will think, and at the same time –' She broke off. 'There's no understanding your granny, sweetheart,' she said to the baby. 'There now, my pretty one. Put her in the cradle, Sukey love. Did Da tell you my own plan?'

'Never a word,' Susannah said, surprised.

'You remember that old dairywoman who hired a couple of rooms in the gatehouse – the Lee Gate – and died, oh, two winters since? She kept a cow in the cellar there, and grazed it in St Stephen's Fields. Well, I walked round to look at the rooms the other day. There's a kitchen with a window opening on Lee Street – she sold cups of milk over the windowsill in summer, you recall – and another room above it with double doors on to the rampart.'

'Yes, I remember. You're not thinking of turning cow-keeper, surely?'

Polly laughed. 'Da will give us a roof over our heads, and Mam will scold me on the one side and spoil the baby on the other,' she said, 'but at the least I should clothe and feed us.

The town's full-provided with coffee-houses and taverns and alehouses where the men can go, and eating-houses and hotels for the wealthy, but there's no place a young couple can spend their free hours, save walking on the walls or in the fields by the river, or sitting in someone else's kitchen.'

'Yes, but . . .'

'If I can hire the gatehouse rooms,' Polly said, 'I'll turn the kitchen into a little dairy with a counter, and sell syllabubs and flummeries and junkets and lemonade. And upstairs I'll have a little parlour opening on the ramparts, where people can sit to drink their bowl of curds or their cup of buttermilk. The cellar would make a good store-room, it's deep dug and the shelves are slate. If Saltings would supply me with milk and cream and eggs, it could work out very well. In Spain, when we could hardly breathe for the dust on one day's march, Mrs Delahunt said to me that she'd give five guineas for a dish of ice cream, the sort the fashionable pastrycooks in London serve to ladies and their escorts in summer. It set me thinking. I could sell Da's custard tarts too, and his almond creams. You look surprised, Sukey.'

'You've worked it all out so trim and tidy. But what would happen come winter?'

Polly laughed. 'Yes,' she said, 'I've begun to think there's a deal of Mam in you. In winter, let me tell you, there's all the more need for a warm dry respectable place where a shopman can buy his girl hot buttered muffins.' She turned her head, smiling at the baby in the cradle. 'Snug and warm as you, my poppet. I mean to ask Cassy to be one of her godmothers, Sukey, and you'll be the other, won't you?'

Susannah said, 'I'd love to be her godmother, but –' She hesitated. 'I thought you might want to ask Barbary.'

'I thought of it,' Polly said, 'and then I thought again. God willing, come peace and Dick's safe return, we'll have a son. And when it's young Richard Fletching's turn to be carried to church, Barbary can be godmother, and relish doing it, with two godfathers to dangle after her. Barbary for the boy.' She lay back against the pillows. 'Is everything ready?'

'I think so,' Susannah said. 'Da's been baking more cradle cake all morning, and Mam's counting the tea-spoons.'

Old Will had hung a garland on the yard gate – ivy for a girl – and was waiting to admit the callers. Cassy and her grandfather were the first to arrive, closely followed by Miss Bagot, who admired the baby from the doorway, refused the cake – 'Too rich for me, I fear, I have to be *so* careful' – and went away again to close the curtains of the windows overlooking the yard. Cassy kissed Polly's cheek and stooped over the cradle. 'She's as pretty as a nosegay.'

'Sukey's going to be one of her godmothers,' Polly said, 'and you'll be the other, won't you, Cassy love?'

Cassy blushed and said shyly that it would make her very happy.

Mrs Oliver came in from the little dining-closet, carrying a pot of tea, and followed by Jonathan with a brimming glass for old Mr Woodling. She nodded approvingly when told the choice of godmothers. 'Who's to be godfather, though?' she asked. 'Kit Tree's a nice lad, but young. Had you thought of Cousin Henniker?'

'They're the same age, Mam, give or take a couple of months,' Polly said. 'But no, neither of them. I mean to ask Abram.'

'Now that's an excellent notion,' Jonathan said warmly.

'So you will have to bake kichel cake, Da,' Polly said, smiling at him. 'Kichel cake for her godparents to give her at her christening.'

Mrs Oliver said, 'We're not done with the cradle cake yet, never mind planning more bakings. Cut a slice for Cassy, Susan. Now, Polly, all this talk of christening brings one question to mind: what's her name to be?'

'Dick wanted to call a daughter after me,' Polly said, 'just as I wanted to call a son Richard after him.'

'So it's Mary?' Mrs Oliver said. 'Very proper.'

Polly said, 'He wanted to – to vary it a little.'

'Molly, you mean? Or Maria?'

'No, Mary, but not Mary alone. A second name – '

'Mary Anne? That's neat enough.'

'Mary Ambree,' Polly said. 'If Parson approves it.'

Mrs Oliver sniffed. 'Mary Ambree? I don't call that a proper name for a Christian child. You realize we'll have the children singing that ballad up and down the street half the night, the moment they know? And chasing after us to the christening, singing it at the tops of their voices? She'll be sung in the streets, poor little scrap, and her not one month old.'

All afternoon friends and neighbours came across the yard to admire the baby, tuck sixpence in her hand or put a bright new penny on the table beside the tea-tray, drink her health and enjoy her cradle cake and ask what her name was to be. The Verneys and the Bullus girls came together, to laugh and exclaim over 'Mary Ambree Fletching'; Fanny Challen from the mill brought a handkerchief worked with ears of corn for luck; Harriet's sister brought a bunch of her wedding ribbons to tie to the cradle. Parson came, and slipped into Polly's hand a note of congratulations from Banker Pratt's nephew, folded round a shining crown piece, and Polly blushed, her eyes very bright. Cousin Henniker kissed her cheek and gave her a little silver sugar-scoop. He backed away hastily when Barbary Chance arrived with a gift from the workroom: a small frilled bonnet made of white muslin, trimmed with ribbons of rifle-man-green and the narrowest silver braid. All the girls exclaimed over its prettiness, though Mrs Oliver looked askance and Pru could only bring herself to praise the neatness of the stitching.

The last of the callers left at dusk – 'And just as well,' Mrs Oliver said. 'Polly needs a good night's sleep. Draw the curtains, Susan, we'll let your sister rest.'

Polly said, 'The children will be coming to sing for the baby, Mam. Wait a while longer.'

Mrs Oliver clicked her tongue. 'I'd clean forgot that. We could pay them their pennies and bid them come back another day . . . No, well, I didn't think you'd care for that. We'll get you and little Mary settled for the night while we're waiting.'

The window overlooked Simnel Street, and it was there that the neighbourhood children gathered to sing for the baby, in hopes of pennies and buns. Several of the boys had brought tin whistles, and one had a small drum tucked under his arm. They sang *The Ballad of Mary Ambree* with great relish, and Susannah leant out of the window to tip a bag of pennies into the pinafore held out by one of the older girls. Jonathan cut up the left-over cake and handed that out as well, and the smaller ones stuffed it in joyfully as fast as they could go.

'Well, that's over and done with,' Mrs Oliver said, getting up and shaking out her skirts. 'Latch the window, Susan, and get the curtains drawn.' She pinched out the bedside candle. 'There now, little one,' she said, rocking the cradle, 'night's come and you should sleep.'

But outside in the dark, their voices thickened by plum cake but gathering strength as they sang, the children were singing again.

Jonathan cocked his head. 'What's that they've chosen?'

'Only one of the street-songs, they crop up year after year,' Mrs Oliver said, plumping the pillows. 'I wish *I* had a penny for every time I've heard that tune. Susan, tell them we'd be obliged if they'd take themselves off now.'

But Susannah too was listening. 'They've changed the

words,' she said, 'the way they sometimes do.'

> *As pretty Polly Oliver lay musing in bed,*
> *A comical fancy came into her head:*
> *'Nor father nor mother shall make me false prove,*
> *I'll enlist for a soldier and follow my love.'*

> *So early next morning fair Polly arose*
> *And dressed herself up in a boy's suit of clothes,*
> *Coat, waistcoat and breeches, and beside her a sword,*
> *And forth she went seeking her outlandish lord –*

Even in the dimness of the parlour, only one candle still burning, Susannah saw her sister's blush. But such stories came into a dozen favourite street songs; the children could not know about the flagship.

> *To the inn where she put up came Polly's true love,*
> *She looked in his face and resolved him to prove,*
> *And he was a soldier, a soldier so fine,*
> *He sat at the board and he called for red wine.*

The boys' voices rang out, taking the soldier's part:

> *'So what do you carry, my little foot-page?*
> *For you are a lad of the tenderest age:*
> *Your locks they are curling, and smooth is your chin,*
> *And your voice like a flute warbles softly and thin.'*

The girls sang in answer:

> *'A letter, a letter, sir, sent by a friend,*
> *And to you 'neath the seal she a gold ring does send:*
> *She saw you, and liked you, one night on the way,*
> *And will give you great riches if with her you'll stay.'*

Jonathan was marking time with a tea-spoon and humming the melody.

138

If a lady did send it howe'er rich she be,
No gold 'neath the seal can commend it to me,
No guineas, no jewels, shall make me false prove,
Nay, I will stay faithful to my own true love –

The baby whimpered a little and Mrs Oliver bent over the cradle to hush her. 'They'll soon be done now, sweetheart, and then you and your Mammy can sleep.'

Now Polly was drowsy, she hung down her head,
And called for a candle to light her to bed:
'My house it is full,' the landlady swore,
'The beds are bespoke, you must lie on the floor.'

Then early next morning this fair maid arose
And dressed herself up in her true woman's clothes,
Up over the stair she so nimbly did run
To he who'd proved constant to his dearest one.

Her Da and her Mam pretty Polly did mourn,
They spent hundreds of pounds for their daughter's return,
But she'd married a soldier who fights for the King
And the life of a soldier's a dangerous thing.

The last verse brought a touch of cold into the room. Susannah shivered at the window, and Polly reached out to the cradle.

Mrs Oliver said, 'I never thought to stand in my own house and hear a daughter of mine sung in the streets. That fairly crowns the day. Close the curtains, Susan, before they start on yet another version. Good night, Polly, sleep well. Good night, little Mary, sweet rest.'

Susannah drew the curtains. The children ran off into the dark, laughing and shouting. She wondered, looking out, when Dick Fletching might come walking up Simnel Street to claim his wife and child, and what the children would sing to welcome him then.

Jonathan had set a cake aside for friends and well-wishers who hadn't been able to call in person, and on the following day, when the baking was over and the bakehouse set to rights, he stood at the table cutting it up and putting the slices in a basket. Susannah rubbed the beechwood marker with a clean dry cloth, and put it away in the Bible box beside the daybook.

'That's right,' Jonathan said, 'See all safe. Your sister tells me the christening's to be on Sunday next. You and Abram had best start baking the kichel cake.'

Susannah hesitated. 'My apprentice piece, Da?'

'If that's what you choose to make it, Sukey love. Though it's not many apprentices have twelve hundred bride-cakes already to their score.'

Susannah smiled. 'Yes,' she said. 'I do choose.'

'And that's good hearing,' Jonathan said. 'I'll speak to your Mam tonight, and tell Abram tomorrow.'

Susannah took the basket and set out to deliver the cake. She went first to Trumper Street, to leave a piece for young Mr Pratt with a note of thanks from Polly; then to the draper's, where Kitty Osborne was in bed with a feverish cold; then to Bell Yard with slices for all Josh's family, Duck Lane for Billy's mother and sister, Tanner's Yard for Sam's widowed mother; and out by the West Gate to Jervis Row, to leave a slice for the aunt with whom Col was lodging. The local militia had been drilling in St Stephen's Fields. As she walked down to the shipyards, she heard the men singing idly as they made ready to march back to town: '*And he was a sergeant, a sergeant so fine, he sat at the board and he called for red wine –*'

She left a slice of cake at the shipyard for the Master Carpenter, and walked on towards the sea, taking the rest to Will's favourite alehouse by the Sea Steps. She went by the sawpits where the smell of sawdust was thick on the air and heard a man whistling the same tune, and going along the Hard she heard it again, this time being sung by the seamen. Their voices carried far across the water on the still cold air:

As pretty Polly Oliver lay musing in bed,
A comical fancy came into her head:
'Nor father nor mother shall make me false prove,
I'll enlist for a soldier and follow my love –'

Susannah climbed the Steps towards the Sea Gate, reckoning that the song might reach the Peninsula quicker than any letter. She smiled, thinking of her mother's likely reaction: *Sung through the streets* was bad enough, *Sung across Spain* would be beyond words. She thought of the Army whistling it as they marched over the mountains into France, and as she walked up Simnel Street she could hear Dick Fletching singing it as he came home from the wars.

Acknowledgements

I am grateful to the authors, representatives of authors' estates, and publishers who have granted me permission to quote from collections of folk song, and in particular to the following: the English Folk Dance and Song Society for 'The Young and Single Sailor', 'All Things Are Quite Silent', 'The Monday March Away' which is taken from 'The Manchester Angel', and 'O Shepherd', from *The Penguin Book of English Folk Songs*, edited by R. Vaughan Williams and A. L. Lloyd (Penguin, 1959); Lawrence & Wishart for 'The Young Seaman' which is taken from 'The Unfortunate Rake', 'Now Christ Was in a Manger Born' which is here assigned to Joseph Gooding, and 'As I Walked Out One Morning', from *Folk Song in England* by A. L. Lloyd (Lawrence & Wishart, 1967); the Cecil Sharp Estate for 'The Cuckoo', 'The Turtle Dove', 'The Lowlands of Holland' (*'I'll build my love a ship'*) and 'High Germany', from *The Idiom of the People* by James Reeves (Heinemann Educational, 1958); Bob Copper and William Heinemann Ltd for 'Come All My Jolly Boys', from *A Song for Every Season*, copyright © Bob Copper 1971 (songs copyright © Coppersongs 1970), reprinted by permission of William Heinemann Ltd.

The bride-cake recipe comes originally from Elizabeth Raffald's *The Experienced English Housekeeper*, first published in 1769. It was sent by the Misses Hope of Reading to Florence White when she was collecting recipes for her book *Good Things in England* (Jonathan Cape, 1932). Florence

White includes a lively description of a test baking and says the cake proved excellent. Recipes for many of the breads, buns and cakes baked by Jonathan Oliver may be found in *Good Things in England,* or Dorothy Hartley's *Food in England* (Macdonald, 1954), or Elizabeth David's *English Bread and Yeast Cookery* (Allen Lane, 1977).

The song 'Polly Oliver' is much older than this story would suggest, and it was being sung at least half a century before my Polly set out.

Harry Smith was an officer in the Rifle Brigade and fought in the Peninsular War. In his *Autobiography* (edited by G. C. Moore Smith, and published by John Murray in 1910) he describes the battle of Waterloo in 1815, which brought the Napoleonic Wars to an end. His brother Charles was sent with a burial party to help clear the battlefield and bury the Regiment's dead. 'In gathering the dead bodies, he saw among the dead of our soldiers the body of a French officer of delicate mould and appearance. On examining it, he found it was that of a delicate, young and handsome female. My story ends here, but such is the fact.'

20309

DATE DUE			